AGR6748
D0801502

THE LONG NIGHT OF LEO AND BREE

Also by Ellen Wittlinger

RAZZLE

* * *

GRACIE'S GIRL

* * *

WHAT'S IN A NAME

* * *

HARD LOVE

THE LONG NIGHT OF LEO AND BREE

Ellen Wittlinger

Simon & Schuster Books for Young Readers
NEW YORK * LONDON * TORONTO * SYDNEY * SINGAPORE

SIMON & SCHUSTER BOOKS FOR YOUNG READERS
An imprint of Simon & Schuster Children's Publishing Division
1230 Avenue of the Americas, New York, New York 10020

Book design by Russell Gordon
The text for this book is set in 12-point Aldine.
Printed in the United States of America
2 4 6 8 10 9 7 5 3 1
Library of Congress Cataloging-in-Publication Data
Wittlinger, Ellen.
The long night of Leo and Bree / by Ellen Wittlinger.
p. cm.
Summary: On the anniversary of his sister's murder, Leo, tormented by his mother's insane accusations and his own waking nightmares, kidnaps a wealthy girl intending to kill her, but instead their long night together helps them both face their futures.
ISBN 0-689-83564-7
[1. Family problems—Fiction. 2. Murder—Fiction. 3. Victims of crimes—Fiction. 4. Emotional problems—Fiction.] I. Title.
PZ7.W78436b Lr 2002
[Fic]—dc21
00-052232

For Kate and Morgan

* * *

Acknowledgments

* * *

Thanks to my editor, David Gale,
his assistant, John Rudolph,
my agent, Ginger Knowlton,

and

Pat Lowery Collins, Suzanne Freeman,
David Pritchard, and Madeline Segal
for their help and advice on the manuscript,

and

Maria DeLuca, for knowing how to save herself.

THE LONG NIGHT OF LEO AND BREE

8:00 P.M.

Leo

She's screaming at me again, like I'm deaf, like I'm stupid, like I don't know what day this is. I knew she'd be crazier than usual today—that's why I got up early and went to work at the garage before she woke up this morning. I figured there was no sense taking a chance—the more I'm around her today, the more likely I'll start seeing those pictures flashing in my mind again.

After work I stopped at the store to get some hamburg and a jar of pickles for dinner because she likes that. I thought maybe I could get her off the subject, get her quieted down with a full stomach. I'm not a great cook, but I can make decent hamburgers. Gramma showed me how. She usually does our cooking, but she's down to Quincy this week with my Aunt Suzanne, who just had another baby. Ma calls Suzanne a frigging baby machine, unless she calls her something worse.

It's bad timing that Gramma's gone this week because sometimes she can get Ma to calm down. I can't. I just make things worse. Which is what she always tells me I do. But I don't think that's fair because I have tried to help out. I quit school this year to work at the garage because she said we couldn't all live on what Gramma made answering the phones at that doctor's office. She said I was eating too much and we couldn't afford it. She bitches at me all the time, even though I help out around here more than she does.

But I know she can't really do anything. She's pretty much nuts most of the time. It didn't used to be like this. Before my sister Michelle died four years ago (four years ago tonight), we didn't live at Gramma's apartment. We still lived in Fenton, but in a regular house with my dad. He worked over at the power plant and Ma worked at a fabric store down on Russell Avenue. We weren't rich or anything, but we were all alive and nobody was insane.

After Michelle died, Dad turned into stone. The rest of us were more like glass, but he was stone. Just sat around the house all day, staring at the wallpaper like he could see down through all the layers. Pretty soon he got fired from the plant and he didn't even seem to care. Then he packed up a duffel bag and told us he was moving down to Kentucky.

"Why? Where?" Ma yelled at him. "You don't know anybody in Kentucky!"

"That's the point," he said. "I can't stand knowin' anybody anymore. I have to disappear." And that's what he did. Although he did send me a birthday card last year with fifty dollars in it, and the post office mark said Louisville, so I guess that's a clue. Maybe someday I'll drive down there and disappear too.

When I was a kid, Dad would take me down to the power plant and show it off to me and me off to the guys he worked with. He was proud of his whole life, it seemed like. But after Michelle died, the rest of us just turned into some broken-down mess. I can't even remember what any of us looked like without a picture.

"Leo! Where are you?" She's still screaming, but I'm downstairs in the basement storage room where she won't find me. I come down here lately when I need to get away—it's a great hiding place. Somebody left an old couch sitting here and some dining room-type chairs. Stuff people aren't using anymore they put down here—there's all kinds of crap: garden tools and suitcases and boxes of old clothes. There's a light in the corner so you can see to do stuff, although usually I don't have much to do, maybe read one of these old magazines people got piled up. It's hard to read, though, when I get Ma's crazy voice stuck in my head, noisy as a chain saw, slicing through my brains.

There's even a toilet behind this door in the back—kind of filthy—but I use it if I don't feel like going back upstairs yet. I bought some toilet paper and some root beer and saltines at the store this afternoon and brought them down here like this was my home. It's kind of cold in the basement, so the root beer doesn't even need to be in a fridge. I'm starting to think of this as *my* place, where I can escape from her and her damn voice. Ma doesn't know this room is here, even though Gramma's apartment is just one floor up. See, Ma never goes outside our apartment anymore; she never even answers the door, so, to her, going down into the basement of the building is like a normal person getting on the space shuttle. No way.

"Leo! Come here this minute! You worthless turd! Come *here*!" She's just getting wound up; she calls me worse than that when she really gets going. I know what she wants. She wants me to sit up there and talk to her, like she isn't a lunatic or something. And I know what she wants to talk about too, but I won't. I'm starting to have those nightmares again anyway—I do every year around this time—other times too, but always in March, and they always get real bad the closer it is to today, March 19. Sometimes the nightmares get so bad I think I might be as crazy as Ma. And sometimes it seems like there's this noise in the corner of my brain—I can't stop listening to it, but I don't know what it is either.

I don't think anybody outside notices, though. I'm pretty careful when I talk to people. The guys at the garage think I'm just this quiet kid who's pretty good with cars. Sometimes I come into work and I feel so mad from the nightmares and from remembering and thinking too much, and my stomach is pitching around so bad I feel like I'm gonna puke, so I don't talk to anybody until I can swallow all that awful feeling way down. I try to joke around with the other guys, but it's hard. They're mostly older and they like to talk about women in ways that . . . well, ways that remind me of Novack.

Michelle was seventeen years old, just like I am now.

She seemed so grown-up to me. She was the person who always made everything all right. When Michelle was around, nobody argued—not me and Ma, or Ma and Dad—she just knew how to get you in a good mood. She had plans to be a social worker, so she could get everybody else in Fenton to settle down too. It probably wasn't too realistic, but that was her hope.

I took Michelle's side against Ma the first time she spent the night at Novack's place. Ma said he was too old for her and a wiseass besides. I argued she was old enough to make up her own mind, even though I didn't like him much myself. I wasn't just arguing for Michelle, though—I was also arguing for me, that I was getting old enough too and wanted to be allowed to make up *my* own mind. When you're thirteen, it never occurs to you there are people in the world rotten enough to kill your sister in a horrible way for no good reason.

Michelle never really had a boyfriend before Novack. She was kind of shy and just average pretty, but really nice. Not the type high school boys are in the market for. At least not around here. She had a job three nights a week working at the gift shop down at the hospital, and one night Novack came in to buy some flowers for his girlfriend, who was laid up in there. (With a broken jaw—but we didn't put two and two together at the time.)

So he starts coming in and talking to Michelle, flirting, and before you know it he forgets all about the poor girl with the wired-shut jaw, which, as it turns out, is lucky for her. He goes in and buys flowers and gives them right to Michelle, right as soon as he buys them from her. Nobody had ever done stuff like that before, and she totally fell for it. I think she was shocked that a guy could really like her. Which was stupid because she was great, and somebody good would have liked her someday if she could have just waited. But I guess she didn't know that.

Right after it happened, I felt like a stick of dynamite with all that explosive powder stuffed in tight. I threw up all the time, but it didn't help; you can't get rid of poison that easy.

Last year on this night, it was pretty bad. Really bad. People keep saying how things will get better—time heals your wounds, or some such crap—but it's not true for me.

What happened last year is that Ma started crying and kept it up all day. Not just regular crying, but drunk crying, crazy crying, nonstop, *put-me-out-of-my-misery* crying. I was trying to read a book for English class, but I couldn't make any sense of it what with Ma's noise and the noise in my own head, buzzing away like a mad, stuck bee that's willing to sting everything in sight to get himself free.

The pictures that usually came to me in nightmares started flashing into my head, even though I was wide awake. Everything was just *pumping* inside me so bad I finally couldn't sit still. I knew if Michelle had been there she could have calmed me down—she could do that even when we were kids—she didn't let stuff get to her like I did, like Ma did. She knew how to talk to you so you didn't feel so bad.

Of course, thinking like that made it all the worse because Michelle could never calm us down anymore now. She was the reason we were all as crazy as we were. So finally I got so mad I didn't know what the hell I was doing—I went crashing into Ma's bedroom like a blind man, and I hit her. I hit her hard, so her mouth started bleeding, but she still didn't stop crying. Gramma heard the noise, which was a good thing because she came in and stopped me. I swear, if she hadn't come in, I was ready to put my hands around Ma's neck and start squeezing off the noise—I was that desperate.

Gramma's more like Michelle was—she can get you to think about what you're doing. After I calmed down a little, she sent me outside and I spent all night just walking around Fenton. I even took my old pocketknife and made some cuts on my wrists, just to see what it looked like, just to feel myself bleed. Man, I hope I never feel that bad again.

I promised Gramma before she left that this year I'd stay down here in the cellar all night—just leave Ma alone with her miserable booze. But even this is way too close.

"Leo! Damn you to hell! *Where are you?*"

I gotta get out of the house. Even a floor down, I

can't stand the screaming. But I need my car keys and they're up there in the kitchen. Shit. She'll jump on me the minute I walk in. I'll just get my coat and my keys and go. I don't like to leave her all alone when she's this bad, but what choice have I got? Either I get out of here or I go loco too.

Bree

I have to get out of here tonight—go someplace by myself. Completely *alone*. I'm sick of listening to all these people trying to convince me what experts they are on my future. What makes them think they know better than me what I should do with my life? It's *my* life!

First I've got Jesse bugging me all afternoon about how great it'll be when we're both at Tufts University next year. He applied early decision, so he already knows he's going there, but I've told him a million times I don't really want to go to Tufts. I only applied there to shut him up, and I only applied to Mount Holyoke to shut my mother up, but they're both still yapping at me, and I don't want to go to either of those schools. They're too close to home.

I want to go someplace far away, someplace different, someplace where *I* can be different. Someplace where people don't have a Lexus *and* a Volvo *and* a big boat parked in the backyard all winter. Oberlin or Grinnell or Reed or Rice. I don't even care so much where it is, just so it's not near *here*. I've lived in Hawthorne for seventeen years; don't I deserve to see what else there is in the world?

But when I say that to Jesse, he takes it as a personal attack and goes ballistic. "If you really loved me, you wouldn't want to go far away! You'd want to stay with me!" God, he reminds me of my mother.

Maybe he's right. Maybe I don't love him enough. I mean, Jesse's a great guy, but we've been dating for almost two years already, which is a lot for high school. Maybe too much. Sometimes I think: Do I really want to spend my whole life with the only guy I ever went out with since I was fifteen? He's always been like this, wanting us to be together every single minute, which at first I thought was so flattering. But now I'm just sick of it. The more he wants to own me, the more I want to get away.

After dinner tonight, I made the mistake of telling my mother about the argument with Jesse, whom she adores. I'm kind of in the habit of telling her things because we used to get along really well and sometimes I forget that we don't anymore. When other girls would complain that their mothers were always crabbing at them, I could never join in. It was actually a little embarrassing how much my mother let me get away with. If there was something I wanted—clothes, CDs, a certain food for dinner, whatever—I just had to ask for it and she'd go out and get it. If I wanted to go to a movie or a concert, she'd drive me and all my friends. All I had to do to earn her slavery was to be a good girl, to stay inside the invisible fence she'd built around my life.

Then last year I joined the Drama Club and got a small part in *Guys and Dolls*, and she took out a full-page ad in the program that said, YOU ARE MY DOLL! LOVE, MOTHER. I guess she didn't think Dad would want to be included in such a public display of affection. Anyway, when I saw that page, it made me feel sick. It suddenly hit me that I *was* her little doll—bought and paid for. I felt like she was always behind me, dressing me up, making me talk, moving me through the life she had planned for me. I decided my days of being a plaything were over. Mother was not amused.

"There's nothing wrong with Tufts" is how she starts her speech tonight. She's finishing her coffee and watching a PBS show about dolphins, which I'm sure she's seen at least three times before. She likes dolphins because "they're so human." Which seems like a dumb reason to like them. *Humans* are human; dolphins are dolphin. Just because they're less likely to take a bite out of your thigh than a shark doesn't make them people. You should like things for themselves, not because they're like *you*.

"Of course if you want a little space from Jesse, Mount Holyoke would be the perfect distance. You could still come home on the weekends—you'll have your car and it's only two hours from here. And since it's all girls, Jesse wouldn't have to worry about you meeting someone else!"

And neither would she. "What if I *want* to meet someone else?" I say.

She shrugs, pretending this possibility doesn't horrify her. "You'll look a long time to find someone as nice as Jesse."

"As rich as Jesse, you mean." His dad is the CEO of some big bank in Boston.

"That is not what I mean. Jesse is bright, he's good-looking, and he has a promising future." She smiles at the TV because some girl in a wet suit is kissing Flipper.

"Yeah, I guess that's the whole package!" I say. "So what if he criticizes everything I say? So what if he has to have the last word all the time? So what if he's got to be in charge of everything, as if I'm some baby who can't cross the street alone?"

"That's just the way men are, Bree. Jesse can give you a secure life," she says, giving me an earnest look. A life as good as hers, she means, with every comfort she could want and a husband who works twelve hours a day and then sits in his den surfing the Net, interacting with strangers rather than speaking to his family.

"Mom, I'm seventeen! I don't want a secure life. Not yet! I want to do things and go places and meet people."

"Oh well." She brushes that notion aside. "You just

need to grow up a little."

"And how am I going to do that if I'm tied to Jesse—I can only grow as much as he grows." And, believe me, growing doesn't interest him. Jesse thinks he's perfect already.

She smiles that infuriating "mother-knows-best" smile. "A tomato plant is staked to a pole in the garden so that it can grow tall and bear fruit. Without support it will shrivel up and drop its bounty on the ground."

I hate it when she starts using gardening analogies. She thinks they're suitable for every situation. If I've got a headache, I'm "droopy as a late-season sunflower." If I've got a test I don't want to study for, she reminds me, "He who works the soil, picks the fruit!" If I complain about the uselessness of taking another year of math, she says, "You can't see the carrots until you dig them up!" It pisses me off to be compared to vegetables.

"I'm not a goddamned tomato plant! You think women have to be 'staked' to men in order to grow? God, you are so prehistoric!"

"If this is the way you talk to Jesse, I'm surprised he wants to have anything to do with you. Lord knows who you'll end up with if you go around screaming at young men the way you scream at me."

She doesn't like raised voices. Especially mine. She likes me to be genteel. Which means: Calm down, do what I say, stay inside the fence. I'm so sick of it. She picks up an *Architectural Digest* from the coffee table and pretends to look through it, but I know she's feeling hurt. Another minute and that pout will turn into genuine tears. I have to get out.

"I'm going for a drive," I tell her, checking that the keys are in my pocket and heading for the coat closet. I've had this little trip in mind since my argument with Jesse this afternoon. If I tell my mother where I'm headed, she'll lie down across the driveway, forcing me to run over her physically as well as metaphorically in order to get out.

She's on my tail in an instant. "Going out? It's late! It's dark!"

"I know it's shocking to you, Mother, but people do actually go outside at night. They actually drive cars after dark."

"Don't speak to me in that tone. Where are you going? Are you meeting Jesse somewhere?"

"I'm not sure," I say, which is a lie. No matter where I end up, I'm quite sure I'm not meeting Jesse there. I pull my black leather jacket off its hanger. It's the look I want with the short skirt, the spandex top, the killer heels.

"You're not going out in that little jacket! It's winter!"

"It's almost spring. And it's not that cold tonight."

She gives me the once-over. "Bree, you're dressed like a . . . a hooker!"

"Oh, for God's sake, Mother. The skirt is from

Tweeds, the jacket is from Ann Taylor. Is that where the hookers you know shop?"

"But you don't dress like this!" She's right about that. I don't usually dress so . . . well, so sexy. But tonight is different. I want to fit in at the bar; I don't want anybody to look at me and think, *She's not from Fenton.* Tonight I'm a shark instead of one of those meek little dolphins. Tonight I'm getting out of Hawthorne. If I can just get out the front door.

"Don't worry so much," I say in my sweetest voice, my hand on her shoulder. "I'm just taking a little drive. I'll be back by ten-thirty." I can see she's about to resist me on the time, so I add: "Next year when I'm in college, at Mount Holyoke or wherever, you won't know where I am at night."

She gives me a rueful little smile as I slip through the door to freedom.

8:30 P.M.

Leo

I've never seen her this bad. I can hear her talking to herself when I sneak up into the kitchen and get my keys. Damn, they jingle a little as I stuff them in my pocket. She hears every noise, like a rabbit or some other little animal that's hoping not to be dinner for a bigger one, so, of course, she's on top of me before I can get out.

She takes it in right away that I've got my coat on. "You're not going out! You can't go out tonight! Don't you have any brains? Don't you know what day this is?"

"I know, Ma," I tell her. "I'm just going down to the garage for a while to hang out with the guys."

Her face twists up in a knot like I said I was going down to Bridgewater to hang out with the criminally insane. "*Guys?* I don't want you hanging out with any *guys.* Men are trouble. You oughta know that. Men with nothing to do and no sense. Next thing they'll be wantin' to go after some girl. Some poor girl. What then?" She pokes at me with this big brown envelope she's holding. She smells like Gramma's liquor cabinet already. Man, I oughta pour all that crap down the drain.

"We're not going after girls." I try to keep my voice light, easy, like I don't know she's ready to explode all over me. "This guy Ronnie is working on his car, this old Chevy. He said I could help him . . ."

"Bullshit! Don't you bullshit me, mister! You don't know anything about cars. Whatayou care about cars?"

I stare at her. What do I care about cars? They're just about the only thing I *do* care about anymore. "Ma, that's what I do all day. When I go to the garage. I work on cars. I fix 'em. I'm good at it. Ronnie says I'm *real* good. Don't you even know what I *do* all day?" I know it's a mistake to take her on, but, God, when your own mother doesn't even know what you do all day, it makes you kind of mad, even if she is nuts.

She looks a little confused at first. "You do? You fix cars? I forgot that." She unplugs the coffeepot and the toaster and then plugs them back in. It takes this little bit of time for it to hit her that I talked back to her. Then she turns on me.

"Don't you tell me what I don't know! I know plenty! And if you fix cars all day, you little smartass, how come they don't pay you for it? You should get a real job, where they pay you! Help out around here once in a while."

I take a deep breath. I've just got to be real nice until I can figure out how to get away. Arguing just makes her crazier. "They do pay me, Ma. Remember? I bought groceries tonight. I made you a hamburger with pickles. Remember?"

She works her mouth back and forth, trying to

remember. "You didn't get any of that macaroni and cheese. I like that kind in the box."

She seems a little calmer, remembering dinner, which I bought and cooked and cleaned up after. A million years ago, I used to just come downstairs and sit at the table with Dad and Michelle and wait for Ma to serve up the food, a whole dinner with meat and potatoes and a vegetable. That's how it used to be. And she'd keep after me until I finished every last bean or piece of broccoli.

Dad had to eat all his vegetables too because Ma said he was our role model. He'd complain about it and say he couldn't wait for us to grow up and move out so he could go back to eating whatever he wanted to. But it was just a joke. I guess he doesn't have to eat broccoli anymore, though.

"I'll get you some macaroni tomorrow. I promise." I take just one step backward, toward the door that leads into the dining room and then the living room and then to freedom. But she knows what I'm up to. She cuts me off, stands in the kitchen doorway so I can't get out. I look at her leaning there, blocking my way, dressed in the same gray pajamas she wears all day long, her crazy hair all scratched around like she's been pulling at it again, her mouth working at chewing up some words she forgot to say. This is my mother, and she's a total lunatic. Just looking at her makes me feel like I've been shot all through with electricity, like I'm being electrocuted. My

fingers start to twitch and I bite down on the insides of my cheeks.

"I got something to show you," she says in a teasing voice, like little girls use on the playground in elementary school when they want the boys to stop running around and pay attention to them. Her mouth curves up like something's funny. "Wait till you see what I got. You haven't seen these for a long time."

I turn around and walk across the kitchen. If she isn't going to let me leave, at least I don't have to stand right next to her. She smells like bad breath and dirty sheets and everything you want to forget about human beings.

She opens the brown envelope and takes out a bunch of papers and waves them in my direction. Or, no, it looks like pictures. Oh, God, it couldn't be *those* pictures. How could she have gotten *those*? The lawyers had them. They wouldn't let her . . .

"I think we should take a look at your sister tonight. It's her anniversary, you know. She'd like us to remember her tonight." She walks toward me, holding up an 8x10 photograph of my sister's naked body with fifty-seven stab wounds in it and her neck slashed.

"Remember Michelle?" she says in her little girl voice.

I grab the picture and slam it facedown on the counter. "Where did you get these?"

Now she's holding up another one, another view,

and I remember the last time I saw these pictures, in the courtroom three and a half years ago. That bastard Novack was sitting there with this little grin on his face while they projected all twelve photographs, one at a time, onto a big screen so the whole jury could see them. And we could too. The lawyers had told Ma I shouldn't go that day, but she wouldn't let me out of her sight. She was keeping me safe, she said.

"On this one, you can see her face," she says now, pointing. "He didn't stab her face. That was good. He wanted her to look nice for the pictures."

Novack had taken the pictures himself. They weren't police photos; they were killer photos. When they asked him why he'd taken them, he shrugged and said he thought he might want to show somebody sometime. They were like souvenirs to him. Novack wasn't crazy though; he was just plain evil. How I know is because every day when they led him into the courtroom all chained up in his orange jumpsuit, he'd look over at Ma and Dad and me, and he'd smile at us. A show-off kind of smile, like he was saying, *I showed you.* Ma and Dad tried never to look at him, but I couldn't help myself. I looked at him so my eyes could send him a shitload of the ugliest hate he ever saw. The bastard's still alive—alive and evil and sitting in some prison cell smoking a cigarette, probably, figuring out how to get parole.

Michelle never smoked a cigarette in her life.

"On this one, you can see what a nice shape she had. Michelle was so beautiful." My mother is smiling like these are prom pictures or a wedding or something.

I grab them out of her hands, but I can't help looking at one or two for just a second. Even though I haven't seen them in years, they're familiar. They're in my dreams all the time. Except in the dreams they aren't photographs; in the dreams I'm seeing the real thing. I'm standing there watching Novack kill her, watching him stab that knife into her body fifty-seven times and cut her throat open, and I can't do a goddamned thing about it. I'm like a statue. I'm frozen. Michelle is screaming and I stand there watching like some pissy little coward. When I wake up from this dream, I wish I was dead.

"You shouldn't have these pictures!" I yell at my mother. I'm mad now. I can't help it. How can you be calm when your own mother is looking at bloody pictures of your stabbed sister and talking about how "beautiful" she is?

She shrugs. "I've always had them. Nobody else wanted them."

"Why would *you*? They're horrible!" I take the rest of them out of her hands and throw them behind me on the counter.

Her face gets all red then and she sticks it right up into my face before she screams. "Don't you know who this is? It's my *daughter*! This is all I have left of her!"

She grabs for the photos again but I do too, and we each end up with a handful of them.

I don't want to, but I glance again at the ones I'm holding. They're not focused very well—either Novack was nervous or he didn't even know how to use a camera—but you don't need sharp focus to see how much blood poured out of her body or how terrified she was when she died. I throw the damn things on the floor and grind at them with my boot. Now that I've actually seen them again, I know I'll never get rid of them. Already they're flashing up on the screen in my mind, one after the other, so I can hardly even see what's really in front of me.

I can hear, though. I can't help but hear.

"I told her not to go with that sonuvabitch! I told her she couldn't trust him!" She's crying now and pulling at her hair.

I put my hand out, but I don't really even know where she is because I'm seeing those fifty-seven stab wounds and I'm counting them up. Like in my dream. Twenty-seven, twenty-eight, twenty-nine . . . there's too many . . . I can't find them all . . . I can't. . . .

All of a sudden she's beating on me with her fists. "Why didn't you stop her? You could have stopped her! What's wrong with all of you men? You can't do anything! You're all worthless, you're no good . . ."

"Ma, stop it!" I try to grab her arms, but she's totally wild now and I can't stop her from hitting me.

". . . every one of you! You and your father are just like the rest! You hurt women! Beat us up, kill us, leave us behind to die!"

"Ma, that's crazy! Dad never hurt anybody. All he did was get the hell out of here. And who can blame him for that? I don't."

Now she goes into orbit. The screaming is so loud I figure the police will get a call any minute. "He killed me! Don't you know that? He killed Michelle too! And . . . and *you* killed Michelle too!" She gets this horrible look on her face, and then she picks up a big metal spoon from the counter and starts hitting me with it. "You *killed* her!"

I've got my arms up over my face to protect myself. "Don't say that, Ma," I tell her. "You *know* I never hurt Michelle. Why do you say stuff like that?"

"All of you men killed her! You're all the same. You're all killers!"

I'm yelling at her to stop hitting me, but she won't. I've never seen her this far gone before. I try to run past her for the door, but she trips me, she sticks out her leg and *trips* me, my own mother. And then while I'm on the floor, she's hitting me on the head, hard, with that damn spoon. So there's a drawer right in front of me and I open it to look for something to hit her back with, to make her back off. That's all I'm thinking—if I can hit her back, she'll stop.

And it's the knife drawer. So I take out a big knife,

the one Gramma uses to cut up chicken, to slice through the bones. I'm lying on the floor on top of the pictures of my carved-up sister whose lousy death is now carved permanently into my brain, and my mother is cracking my head open with a metal spoon and calling me a killer. And I grab this knife and jump to my knees, and I swing it at her, swing it right at her chest while she's hollering what a sonuvabitch she always knew I was.

"I knew it! I knew it! You killed her and now you'll kill me too! Do it! Go ahead and kill me too! I want you to kill me like you killed her!" She's backed up against the cabinets with her arms up in the air so I can get a good aim at her heart.

I'm swinging the knife around like crazy because I'm half-nuts now too. "I didn't kill anybody!" I tell her. "It was Novack, not me!"

But she's still yelling at me to kill her, and then I feel my fist tighten on the knife. Maybe, I think, I'll do it. So I can stop her. Stop the yelling and the hating and the sickness. I'm not going to be the one who gets killed anymore. I'm going to be the killer. Just like she wants me to be.

And I think the thing that stops me is the glitter of her wedding ring. Which she usually doesn't even wear anymore, but, for some reason, she has it on now, and it's shining, and it reminds me of when I was a kid how she'd sit and talk to me before I went to sleep, and I'd always want to look at the ring because it was so pretty and her hands were pretty too. And when I notice the ring, I remember she's still my mother, even though she's out of her mind.

I run out through the dining room and the living room into the dark, quiet night where nobody's screaming. I leave her standing there by the cabinets, waiting to die.

Bree

I'm out! I'm free! And alone too. No Jesse to tell me what I should and shouldn't do. I drive south through Hawthorne, past the Beach Club, past my friend Caitlin's house with its eight bedrooms and six bathrooms for three people, past the Unitarian Church and through the little downtown: Ben & Jerry's next to the Antique Emporium next to the LWG. (It's really called Emiline's Boutique, but Caitlin and I call it the LWG for Ladies Who Golf.)

On the other side of town, the houses get smaller and closer together, but they still look nice. They have window boxes and little vegetable gardens in the side yards instead of huge perennial beds you need a herd of gardeners to take care of. But I'm not stopping here either. I leave Hawthorne behind as I cross Elmhurst Avenue. I'm going to Fenton.

People in Hawthorne act like Fenton doesn't even exist. Even though there's just this one street that divides them. And it's not like you can see some big difference when you cross from one side of Elmhurst to the other. The houses all look pretty much the same, small places built close to the street or duplexes with TVs shining in the living room windows on two floors. But they look fine, not run-down or anything.

Of course, as you get into downtown Fenton, there are some shabby-looking places. Fenton isn't a big city; it's one of those towns that used to have mills and shoe factories and employ a lot of people. The factories closed down decades ago and now there are just a lot of big empty buildings with the glass broken out of the windows and people who don't know where else to go or what else to do. And the schools aren't very good and there are kids hanging out on the streets, getting in trouble. Not a terrible place, just a place where there's not much money and people seem kind of confused.

Here's a weird thing: I had never even been *in* Fenton until I was fourteen years old, even though I grew up in the town right next to it. My parents never even drove *through* the place. If we were going somewhere on the other side of Fenton, we'd drive around it on the highway. I used to have nightmares when I was little, with the usual monsters and bad guys in them, and they always took place in Fenton, or at least, what I imagined Fenton must be like: some dark, hideous, haunted place with people waiting at every corner to jump out and get you.

When I got to high school, my freshman social studies teacher, who I thought was very cool, was recruiting kids to work a couple of nights a month at the Main Meal, a soup kitchen in Fenton. The whole idea seemed sort of exotic and *dangerous* to me (and I'd be driving over with that adorable teacher), so I signed up. I was so surprised that first time we drove there, especially after my mother made me promise that I'd lock the car doors while I was *in* the car with the teacher, as though we'd be mobbed by gangs the minute we showed our wealthy faces. *This* was Fenton? Yeah, it was kind of crummy-looking in places, but it wasn't anything like the hell-mouth I'd been imagining.

I got to really enjoy working at the Main Meal. This year I'm the coordinator of the high school program, so I go there all the time. I know some of the guests really well by now (we always call the people who come for dinner guests) and they look for me so we can sit and talk after the serving's done. Oh sure, some of them are kind of crazy, but most are only low on cash and glad for a free meal. And a few of the guests are a little angry and resentful of us rich kids, but most people just act like it isn't at all strange for a bunch of Hawthorne High School students to be dishing out their Monday night spaghetti and meatballs.

Of course I never go into Fenton for any other reason—there aren't any movie theaters or much else to go for. But one Friday night a few months ago, Jesse and I were tired of doing the same thing every weekend, and we were trying to come up with something different. He said his cousin had once taken him to this bar in Fenton that was kind of cool; maybe we should go there. It was just this working-guy's kind of place. His cousin had gotten him a beer with no hassle, and then they'd played pool with some guys. Jesse said, "I guess your mother would have a fit if I took you there."

Well, that did it. Of course, my mother would have a fit, but who was going to tell my mother? It sounded perfect. A bar in downtown Fenton, a working-guy's bar, forbidden, but not really dangerous, an adventure. So we went and we had the best time! The bartender gave us this rolled-eye look when we ordered beers and said, "One. That's it. If you're twenty-one, I'm eighty-one." But he was cool about it. And then we did find some people to play pool with, two guys and a girl a few years older than us. I'd never played before, but they were nice and tried to teach me how to hold the pool cue and not rip up the table with it. I'm not sure why it was so much fun; maybe because I liked feeling I could fit in there, that I was more than just a rich Hawthorne girl.

When I told Caitlin where we'd gone, she couldn't believe it. "You went to a bar in *Fenton!* Are you nuts?

People get killed over there all the time!"

"Oh, they do not!" I said. "You've never even been there."

"Why would I go there? They do drug deals right out in public."

"As opposed to in the bathrooms at Hawthorne High School, you mean?"

Emily Winters was standing there listening to our conversation and squirming with excitement. "I think you're really brave, Bree. God, I'm scared to death to go to Fenton." She thought it over. "Maybe we could get a whole bunch of kids to go to that bar together. That would be a rush!"

I shook my head. "That would defeat the purpose. I don't want to *take over* the bar; I want to be part of it."

"God," Emily said. "I never knew you were so fearless."

Caitlin had another viewpoint. "I never knew you were so stupid."

Ever since then, I've been trying to get Jesse to go back with me again, but he never wants to. That's what we were arguing about this afternoon. He says he feels too responsible for me if we go to a dangerous place.

"But it wasn't dangerous," I tell him.

"Not that time," he says. "We were lucky."

"What could happen? We'd be beaten to death with pool cues?"

"You never know. You think just because you hand

out free burgers at the Main Meal you're protected? Fenton is a crazy place."

I swear, my mother is brainwashing him. I've given up trying to force him to go with me, but that doesn't mean I'm spending *my* whole life in Hawthorne. If Jesse won't go with me, I'll go by myself. Something tells me the bartender will give me a beer, and there'll be somebody at the pool table to play a couple of games with a beginner.

It was right around here someplace, just a few blocks past the Main Meal. But was it Fieldstone Street or Amesbery? The place didn't really have a name, just a beer sign in the window. I'm pretty sure it was off Wilson Avenue. Damn. If I came here more often I'd know where I was.

It's too hard to drive and search at the same time. I'll park the car and get out. It's got to be right here somewhere.

9:00 P.M.

Leo

Can't get calmed down. I'm driving around in circles, going nowhere. When I first got into the car, I couldn't even breath. Thought I might be dying. Hoped I was. That would have been the easy way out. I almost drove down to the garage; Ronnie's down there tonight. But then what? I can't tell anybody about this, and he'd know something was wrong seeing me so messed up. I feel like I couldn't even speak to him, like my vocal chords wouldn't work if I tried.

I can't go back home anymore—I *can't*. Ma called me a killer and I pulled a knife on her! She's totally nuts now and she's got those pictures. I shouldn't be driving—the pictures keep flashing up in front of me, like they were pasted on the windshield. Can't see where I'm going. I turned on the windshield wipers before I realized what I was doing, but wiper fluid won't wash them away. No. I have to keep driving because what will I do if I stop?

Think of something else. Forget the pictures. Think about . . . the car. My Caddy that used to belong to Ronnie. It's old, but Ronnie kept it up, and even gave it a paint job before he sold it to me. I pay it off thirty dollars a week when we get our checks. I try to take good care of it so it'll last me a long time. Except sometimes I don't think anything lasts a long time.

Damn those pictures! Four years ago tonight, that slimeball Novack decided my sister wasn't gonna last a long time. Sliced her up and let her bleed, for no good reason on earth. Oh sure, he said she didn't love him anymore—why *would* she?—and the asshole lawyers argued it was a "crime of passion," but Novack didn't have any passion. He just had stupid hate. He's just one of those dumb bastards who has to screw up everything he touches.

Fifty-seven times. They kept repeating it at the trial. Fifty-seven times he stabbed her. Who does the counting on stuff like that? Is that a job somebody has, to count up stab wounds on dead people? Fifty-seven.

Men are no good—that's what Ma says. She's crazy, but still, sometimes I think she's right. Guys are different. You're not supposed to say that, but I think it's true. Girls talk to somebody when they're mad—guys just smash something up. Just hit it! Hurt it! Kill it! Fifty-seven times! We've got too much anger to let it out in just words.

I feel that way now, like I'm ready to boil over. Can't think straight. Brain noise is getting louder and louder, and the muscles in my arms are jumping around like they're going someplace without me. If only I'd gone over there with her that night, *I* could have killed *him*. Then I'd be in jail, but it would still be better than this.

Crime of passion for sure. Michelle would be alive, and Dad might still live home instead of being lost somewhere in Louisville, and I'd be the one thinking about my parole. And maybe Ma wouldn't be nuts. And maybe I wouldn't either.

That picture again—the one where her head's laying in a puddle of raspberry Jell-O—that's what Mom told me it was back then. Like I was a moron. Like she'd be dead if a little dessert leaked out of her. Can't shake that damn picture! Go away!

Goddammit! I just about hit some guy crossing the street. Can't see right. Gotta get off Wilson Avenue and drive where there aren't so many people. I don't care about the people, though. I really don't.

Fifty-seven times. Even looking at those damn pictures, you can tell she was a nice girl. No pierced eyebrows. No tattoos. No ratty-looking hair or makeup. If she was wearing her clothes, you'd see they were nice too, long skirts and jackets. She looked like she oughta work at a bank or someplace. Not like some of the slutty types you see.

Like over there. There's one. Walking around alone in this crappy neighborhood with two yards of leg sticking out from under her skirt, wearing those fuck-me shoes. Advertising for it. Michelle never did that. Never. Somebody oughta teach that bitch a lesson. It's not fair.

Bree

God, I'm freezing. If I'd known I'd have to walk all over Fenton, I'd have worn a coat. I can't believe I can't find the place. Did they go out of business in two months? It was right *here*. Somewhere.

My mother would die if she knew I was walking around this neighborhood by myself. I'll admit I'm slightly freaked out, but I wouldn't be if I didn't live such an overprotected life in Hawthorne. What am I afraid of? Empty storefronts? Trash in the gutter?

Jesus, there's a car stopping . . . full of guys. I should just ignore them or get off the street somewhere . . . but where? There's no place to go inside!

"Hey, Sis," one of them calls to me. I keep on walking, my eyes fixed on the building at the end of the street, like I know where I'm heading. Maybe if I can get around the corner . . .

The car follows me, backing down the street. How can this be happening? "Lady!" the guy calls again. I walk faster—I'm deaf. "You seen a little brown mutt around here?" he says. "Red collar?"

Gradually I slow down. They're looking for a dog. My heart is pounding and it's hard to get my breath. "Your dog?" I ask.

"My kid brother's mutt ran away. You seen any dogs?"

I shake my head. "Sorry. I haven't."

"Okay. Thanks." He salutes me and the car speeds up again, disappears around the corner.

For God's sake, I've let my mother and all her crazy fears turn me into a complete coward. I'm shaking like a bowl of Jell-O . . . over nothing! I feel like an idiot.

Haven't I learned *anything* from working at the Main Meal? Do I really think people are so different, just because I've crossed from one town to another? A bunch of guys looking for a dog. I hate that I'm programmed to be afraid of people unless they're exactly like me. I won't be that way. I *won't*.

Part of the problem is I've been with Jesse for so long and we go almost everywhere together—I forgot what it's like to just walk around by yourself. You see things differently when you're alone. You use all your senses instead of relying on the other person to point things out. I'm just realizing that when Jesse's with me, I fall back and let him make the decisions. Not all the time, of course, but I always know I don't have to think about things if I don't want to. I don't have to take any responsibility.

Which isn't fair. To me or to Jesse. That's the problem with being a couple. Somebody turns into the leader and the other person becomes the follower. It just happens. And the leader always *has* to be responsible and the follower never *gets* to be. And I'm tired of being the follower. I want to walk around alone for a while and be responsible for myself. Even if I get lost now and then.

9:15 P.M.

Leo

I have to pull over. Can't drive anymore. Even if I close my eyes and push at them with my fists so that orange stars burst out of the blackness, I can still see the pictures. I'm blind and I'm crazy. I'll never be right anymore. Still got the chicken knife here on the seat next to me. I should use it—cut myself—get the whole thing over with this time. The whispery voice in the back of my head—I think that's what it's telling me to do.

If only Ma hadn't had those pictures! If she wasn't a lunatic. If Novack hadn't stabbed my sister fifty-seven times and slashed her throat. If I could go back and change things. If I hadn't let her go over there that night. If I'd talked her out of it. If I'd sided with Ma about what a worthless scumbag Novack was. If he'd met some other girl instead of Michelle. If he'd killed some sleazy girl who deserved it. Then we'd all be okay. It would be the way it was and we'd be okay.

If he'd killed some girl like *that* one. That same stupid girl I saw wandering around here fifteen minutes ago with her skirt up to her ass. Still begging for it. It's funny; when I look at her, I see *her,* not the pictures. She makes them go away. She replaces them in my brain. No. She *becomes* the girl in the pictures.

The voice in the corner of my brain is talking again, and this time I know what it's saying. I pick up the knife and slide across the seat. I don't have to think what to do next—I just know. I wait until she walks just a little past the car and then I open the door and grab her from behind, hold the knife to her throat, and pull her backward into the car before she knows what's happening.

"You're the one who was supposed to die," I tell her. "Not Michelle."

Bree

Oh my God! What the hell . . . ?

"You're the one who was supposed to die. Not Michelle."

Somebody is . . . "Let me go!" I'm in a car! Somebody . . . my neck! "Stop it! Let me go!"

Can't move my head—try to get out . . . an arm reaches around me, slams the door closed. Is it those guys? The ones looking for the dog? I think it's just one person. Oh, my God, *what the hell is going on?*

"Please!" Scream. Scream loud. "Please let me go! Please!"

"Stop yelling or I'll cut your throat," he says. I can feel a knife on my neck. Oh, Jesus! His voice sounds scared, but the knife isn't shaking. Can't breathe. Think, Bree, think!

"What are you doing?" I say, trying to sound halfway normal, slightly annoyed. Maybe this is a joke; maybe it's just someone I know. Trying to scare me. I try to turn around to get a look at him.

He smacks me in the back of the head. "Don't turn around. Nothing to see back here."

Tears squirt up into my eyes. My heart is banging against my jacket. "Don't hurt me. Please. You don't even know me."

"That's one good thing," he says.

"I don't even live here. I live in Hawthorne." Why did I say that? Do I think that will give me immunity? Girls from Hawthorne shouldn't be killed in Fenton? "Do you want money? I don't have much, but . . ."

"Shut up," he tells me.

"You can have the money. Please let me go! I won't tell anybody . . ."

"Shut up!"

"You aren't going to hurt me, are you? Please don't! Please let me . . ." My voice is careening up and down the scale now, out of my control.

"Shut up! I don't want to hear one more stupid word out of your mouth. Sit there and cry and don't give me any trouble while I drive."

He drives with one hand on the wheel and the other around my neck, holding the knife. I'm staring out the passenger side window watching Fenton roll by. There's the bar with the beer sign in the window. I do what he tells me: I cry, but I don't make a sound.

9:30 P.M.

Bree

He doesn't say anything while he drives and I try to think. Which is almost impossible because basically my brain is just quietly screaming, like the rest of me. But there's nobody here to think for me, so I force myself to try. If I die it will kill my mother. It will just kill her. And it will be my own stupid fault. I can't just sit here doing nothing, waiting to be murdered. Maybe he's going to rape me—do rapists usually kill you afterward? While we're driving, past the bar, and past the Main Meal, and down some streets I don't recognize, I'm trying to brainstorm some way out.

Right away I remember that self-defense class I took last year. Mom forced me to take it and I talked Caitlin into going with me, but we just goofed on it and drove the teacher nuts. God, why am I so stupid? They taught you things to do, ways to get away from people in a situation like this! It seemed so silly at the time, all that kicking and yelling. All I remember now is something about poking two fingers in the attacker's eyes—Caitlin and I got hysterical over that, pretending we were the Three Stooges. I'd have to be double-jointed to reach this guy's eyes anyway.

Why can't I remember what to do? I know you're

supposed to use your elbows and knees alot, but just *how* to use them I don't know. When Caitlin and I were supposed to practice grabbing and throwing each other around, we'd just start dancing a tango or a minuet or something. Sometimes we'd get somebody to laugh, but basically nobody in the class liked us much. They were all so *serious* about it. Why wasn't I?

Wait, there is one thing I remember—about dealing with crazy people! I remember this—and it doesn't even have anything to do with fighting. The teacher said if you ever found yourself with a real crazy person, you could try to talk your way out of being killed by . . . by becoming real to them. I remember that was how she put it: You make yourself *real*.

She had this story about a woman who'd been abducted and had told the guy all about her three kids, and how she was going back to school to get her nursing degree, and all about her divorce and everything. It sounds bizarre, but I guess it worked. He let her go. At least, that's the story.

The teacher said that somebody who's crazy enough to want to kill you or rape you isn't thinking of you as a real person. They just see you as BODY or WOMAN or something. So if you make them see that you're a real human being, they might come to their senses and not hurt you. I remember now—the thing you were supposed to do was keep talking about yourself. Just don't shut up.

But when you're this scared, how do you talk? He's stopping the car in a parking lot behind a condemned-looking school building. There are weeds as high as the car growing up around the sides of the lot, so nobody can see us. He turns the engine off and we just sit there silently, not even moving, like some couple on their first date who don't know what to say to each other. Except most boys don't hold a knife to your throat on the first date.

Finally I make myself say something. "Um, I work at the Main Meal sometimes. We passed it back there. You . . . you know the place?"

"I told you to shut up."

"I'm the director of my school's program. We go every other Monday . . ." I hardly even know what I'm saying. I can barely breathe. But at least I'm doing something.

"I don't take handouts," he says. "I work for my meals."

"Oh. Where do you work?" I ask politely, as if we were having a real conversation.

He's quiet a minute, then growls at me. "Like I'm going to tell you where I work. You think I'm an idiot?"

"No! Not at all! But . . ." Keep talking! ". . . I had a job last summer at a camp up in Maine. I taught swimming and horseback riding. Mostly to the little kids . . ."

"Shut up!" He smacks me again in the back of the head and this time I bite my lip, hard. I start to cry again

and I'm thinking that's probably not the right thing to do. How do I know what's right?! My mouth is bleeding and it seems like the beginning of things that are going to hurt. There's enough blood coming from my lip that some of it drips onto the guy's sleeve, the one around my neck.

"Blood," I say. Just the one word because now I'm afraid to talk. I don't know if I'm telling him or telling myself.

Leo

This is the right thing. It must be. She was in the pictures instead of Michelle. She's the one who should have been with Novack that night. Somebody like this deserves what she gets. Now that she's in the car, though, I feel weird.

After I park behind the old school, she starts yakking at me, like I'm her boyfriend or something. I have to hit her a little bit to shut her up—nothing at all like Novack hit girls, like he messed them up—but her lip starts bleeding and it gets on my coat. It's just a few drops, but when they hit the fabric, they spread out like flowers, like a red bouquet. I can't stop looking at it. I hurt her. I made her bleed. I never did that to anybody before.

Even though I have to kill her, I don't like hurting her. I wasn't thinking about the blood.

"How come you're walking around here by yourself?" I ask her, even though I hate it when she talks, when I have to listen to her shaky voice. I ask because I feel bad about hurting her.

She takes a few deep breaths before she answers me. "I was looking for this place my boyfriend took me once, but I couldn't find it."

"Your boyfriend?"

"Yeah." Then she starts in again. "His name is Jesse. We're always arguing lately because he wants me to go to the same college he's going to and . . . and I don't want to. My . . . my mother wants me to go to this school called . . ."

"Okay. Shut up now. So I don't have to hit you again."

That quiets her down, so I can try to figure out what to do next. If there's going to be blood, I don't want her in my car. I need to *think* about this, but I can't—my brain is too messed up from the pictures. Then she says, "If you hurt me, it will kill my mother."

Her *mother*. I didn't think of her having a mother. All of a sudden *my* mother's back in my brain, shrieking about how I killed Michelle. How can she say something like that? I never hurt anybody. Except this stupid girl. And I'm only doing this for Michelle.

"I'm her only child. She's always afraid when I go out. She told me not to go out tonight."

I tighten my grip on the knife at her throat, so she knows I don't care about her or her mother. "She ever tell you not to dress like a whore?"

I can feel her throat swallowing. "Yes."

"I guess you should have listened to her."

"I thought I looked fine. This is an expensive skirt." I lose track of what she's saying, like the soundtrack is muted. She puts her hand to her lip where I split it. I didn't break her jaw, though, like Novack would have. "What are you going to do to me?" she wants to know.

"I told you." But now I'm thinking: How can I do it? I've never done anything like this before. I don't know how. I only know about piston rings and camshafts and cylinder heads—I don't know how you stop a human being from living. But the voice in my head is . . . is *Michelle*—and she's telling me to do it. Because Novack killed the wrong person.

"My father and mother hardly even speak to each other anymore. They talk to me, though. I'm the only reason they stay together. I glue them together. Without me . . ."

"Stop tellin' me all this stuff! I don't give a damn about your parents."

"You should know the consequences of your actions."

That would have made me laugh if there was any laughter left in me. "Nobody knows that," I tell her. "You think you do, but it's not true. You don't even know you're making a mistake and all of a sudden, everything's changed. Everything's wrong. And you can never go back and fix it."

She's quiet for a minute and then she says, "I guess you're right about that."

"Yes, I am. Yes, I am."

10:00 P.M.

Leo

I have to get her out of my car. Too much talking in that little space. Maybe she's crazy too, this girl. I start driving again, and now she says don't worry, she won't look at me—I don't have to keep the knife on her throat. I do anyway, driving one-handed. Why should I trust her? Then she tells me how she's an only child. She wants to know if I have any brothers or sisters. Like she *knows* about it.

"You tell me," I say. "You're so smart. What happened to my sister?"

"Your sister? I don't know. What did happen?"

The pictures flash up again and I shake my head to get rid of them. "She's gone" is all I say.

"Is she . . . dead?"

I don't say anything for a minute, but I miss the corner I wanted to turn. "Are you deaf? I told you to shut up!"

"You don't have to tell me," she says, which is pretty obvious, since I'm the one with the knife. "I had a sister who died too."

I turn and stare at the back of her head. I haven't really looked at her much. She has reddish-brown hair. It's that real clean-looking kind that swings around, the kind you mostly find on rich girls. "You liar. You just said you were an only child."

"I am, now. She died when we were little. I don't remember her very well."

"How old was she?" I don't really want to know about it, but I ask anyway.

"Two, I think. I was about six. I guess I should remember more than I do. I was just a little kid."

"Lucky you." I'm not going to cut her throat. There's too much blood. I have to get her out of the car, so I can stop driving and figure this out. While I'm thinking where to take her, she says, "I haven't seen what you look like. If you let me go, I couldn't identify you."

That's something I hadn't thought about. I mean, she can't ID me if she's dead, but if she got away or something. . . . And anyway, I don't want her looking at me.

I have my bandanna in my pocket, the one I use at work. It's greasy, but I can't help that. I pull the car over and tie the thing tightly around her eyes and triple knot it in the back. She makes a little squeaking noise, which I think means it's too tight. Too bad. I have to start getting tough.

Bree

The last thing I saw before he tied the rag over my eyes was a phone booth under a streetlight. It was like a little piece of hope, that phone booth. It reminded me that I was still in the same world I'd always been in, that if I could just get over there and drop a quarter in the slot, I'd be talking to my own mother in thirty seconds. She always keeps the cordless phone next to her when she's in the living room, so she doesn't have to get up and go into the kitchen. Dad never answers the phone; he says he spends too much time at work on the phone and there's no one he cares to talk to in his off-hours. And he really means *no one*.

And then just as I'm imagining shutting myself into that miraculous booth, the lights go out altogether. For a second I don't know what happened, but then I figure it out. I shouldn't have said that about identifying him. Now I've got this awful-smelling rag over my face. And it's too tight. My eyes hurt.

I thought it was bad before, but now I'm more scared than ever. Where am I? I can't see!

I thought the talking thing was starting to work, making myself real. But he didn't let me go. And now I'm thinking: He probably already killed his sister! He's driving too fast. Maybe I'll faint—I wish I would. With my heart racing so fast, and the stink of this thing over my eyes, I can hardly breathe. My head falls to the side, against the seat.

The car stops.

"Where are we?" I ask, but I don't expect an answer.

He leans over and opens the passenger door and the cold air comes whooshing in. I'm really shaking now, shaking like crazy. He's right behind me as he pushes me out the door. I'm barely on my feet before he's dragging me off somewhere, and I'm stumbling because I can't see anything and because I'm too scared to walk. Where am I walking? I can still feel the knife on my neck only now it's cold, like the wind got right inside it as soon as it could.

"Be very quiet," he whispers. "If you aren't quiet, I'll have to stick you right now. If you're quiet . . . maybe we can talk."

"Okay." Suddenly I can't imagine talking. I tried it and it didn't work. I just want to go home! I want this to be over!

"Eight steps down," he says. He's holding me from behind, which is good because otherwise I know I would just fall down those eight steps. My knees have become unglued.

There's the sound of a heavy door being shoved open, and then he pushes me inside. It's quiet; there's no more wind.

"We're home," he says. And the door closes behind me.

10:30 P.M.

Bree

God knows where we are. It's freezing in here and it smells musty. A basement, I guess. It's quiet, except for a noise that sounds like a furnace coming on, a furnace that heats someplace else.

I'm sitting on some kind of couch and he's tied my feet and hands with ropes, or probably clothesline, so he doesn't have to hold the knife right on me. Which is better. I can breathe better without the knife on my throat. I realized after I got in here that I still had my purse with me, and I tried to think if there was something in there I could use as a weapon. This purse is stuffed with junk, but there's nothing useful. Poke him with a pencil? Shoot him with rubber bands? I don't think so. Why am I so helpless?

I don't know what he's doing, but I can hear him shuffling around; he keeps mumbling like he's talking to somebody, but I don't hear another voice or any other footsteps. He keeps saying the name Michelle. It's almost like he's forgotten I'm here.

I don't know what to do. If I talk, he'll pay attention to me again. Maybe it's better to just sit here quietly. But my self-defense teacher said you *should* talk. He hasn't killed me so far, so maybe she was right.

I try to find my normal voice before I say anything, but I'm not sure I still have a normal voice. "Do you listen to music?" I say finally. "What bands do you like?" Like anybody in my position would care about *bands*.

He stops moving around. I have a feeling he's looking at me. "Bands?" He sounds confused, like he doesn't recognize the word. Or maybe he doesn't recognize *me*.

"Music. Bands. You know."

"You want to know what bands I like?"

Of course I don't, you moron. "Yeah. I was just wondering."

"I don't listen to music. I don't have time," he says.

Too busy with his kidnapping business. "You don't ever go to concerts or anything?"

"I don't waste my money."

So I'm sitting here thinking at least he didn't just say *Shut up* or hit me or anything. At least we're sort of talking. And then he says, "I did go to one once. Last year. I forgot. A friend of mine got tickets and I went."

"You did? What band was it? Where did they play?"

"Why do you care?"

"I'm just interested. You said we could talk."

He grunts. "A band called G4. They were in Boston at Sherborne Center."

I sit up straighter. How weird. "G4? Last year? In the spring?"

"Yeah. I think so. May or June."

"I was there too! I love G4!"

"Yeah? They're not bad. I mean, that was the first time I heard them, but I liked them."

"They rock!"

"Yeah." All of a sudden he sounds totally normal, like some guy from my high school instead of a deranged killer. Which, along with the temperature in this place, makes me start to shiver again. I wish I could take this thing off my eyes and see who this guy *is*. You can tell things from people's faces, like how dangerous they really are, that I can't figure out from just hearing his voice.

"You know why they call themselves G4?" I ask him.

"My friend told me they all have names that start with G. The only one I remember, though, is . . ."

"God." I say.

"Yeah! What kind of person calls himself God?"

"Somebody with a big ego. Greg, Gus, Gordon, and God. Strange," I say, as if anything could be stranger than sitting in this freezer, all tied up, with a handkerchief over my face.

"Probably his real name was Eddie or something, and he just wanted another G-name," he says.

I give a little laugh, which is so forced it comes out sounding like a furball upchuck. He doesn't seem to notice, though.

"I liked them," he says. "G4. I'd go to hear them again."

"Yeah, me too." This normal act is exhausting; my teeth are clicking together.

"Are you cold?" he says.

"Uh, yeah. I'm freezing."

There's a rustling noise like he's taking off his coat. "Here, you can have this." He puts the coat around my shoulders and I can tell it's really big, which makes me think he must be too. Not a comforting thought. But then again, do you warm up somebody you're planning to execute any minute?

"Is this your coat? Couldn't you just turn up the heat?"

"There's no heat down here. I don't mind the cold, though. It keeps me awake. I don't like sleeping anyway."

This conversation is way too bizarre, but I keep talking. "I love going to sleep, especially on a cold night when you can crawl under the heavy covers." Just saying it makes me want to cry. I could be at home right now, getting into my bed with the new Barbara Kingsolver novel, but, no, I had to have my *adventure*.

"I hate sleeping," he says. "I just have bad dreams."

"You do? What about?" Okay, that was probably not a well-thought-out question.

He doesn't answer me, but I hear something crash into the wall and I have a feeling he threw it, whatever it was. "Don't ask me so many questions! You don't even want to know the answers! You think I'm stupid? I know you're just pretending to be nice to me so I'll let you go. But I *can't* let you go! Get it through your head! I *can't!*"

"Okay." I know there are tears leaking out again;

there's nothing I can do to stop them. They get the rag all soppy and it's more uncomfortable than ever. And then all the pretending just stops. I can't do it anymore. I can't be anybody but who I am, a cold, exhausted, very scared person who's afraid she's about to be murdered.

"Okay! I won't be nice to you!" I'm yelling now. "Why should I be nice to you! I hate you! I don't care about your dreams! I just want to go home!"

I can feel the knife again, this time the tip is pushing against my chest. "You have to be quiet," he says very softly. "I'll have to kill you if you keep screaming. If you wake her up, I'll have to kill you right now."

I nod my head and I don't say anything else.

"Why did you make me take her?" he says. "I don't know what to do!" He doesn't get an answer, so I guess he's talking to Michelle again, whoever she is. I guess I don't need to see his face to figure out he's pretty damn crazy.

Leo

I've got the girl down in the basement, in my place down here. I didn't know where else to go, but now I'm afraid she'll make noise and Ma will hear her and start screaming again. I wonder what she's doing up there. I don't hear anything. I hope she just went to bed.

I'm not sure now if Michelle really wants me to kill the girl. I was so sure she did before. I was thinking that I could kind of exchange her for Michelle. And then *she'd* be in the pictures. But how could that happen? The pictures are old, and they're upstairs with Ma. Everybody in that courtroom saw them. I just don't know now.

But I told her I'd kill her, so I guess I have to. I can't let her go. Except I don't know how you kill somebody. *Michelle, I wish you'd tell me what to do!*

And then there's the thing about her sister being dead. Is that true or just some lie she made up so I'd let her go? I think about her mother . . . but it's not the same thing as with Ma. Her sister was little. She was probably sick or something.

"How did your sister die? Was she sick?" I gave her my coat and she's all huddled inside it like we're in Alaska.

"What?" Her head spins around, looking for my voice. "My sister?"

"Yeah, how'd she die?"

"She fell off a wall. It was an accident."

"A wall?"

"At the beach. We were all walking up on a high wall above the sand. It was up around McCormick Island somewhere—I'm not sure exactly—we never went back there afterward. I guess she just slipped and fell. She hit a rocky place. With her head."

"And she was dead right away?"

"I think so. I don't remember too much about it." She rubs her eyes through the bandanna. "Except my mother screaming. I remember that."

So do I. My mother screamed for three solid days after the police came and told us about Michelle.

"What was her name? Your sister."

"Her name was Summer."

"Summer? That's not a name."

"Well, it was *her* name." She sounds kind of mad about it. "My parents went through a hippie phase before they decided to cop out, get rich, and turn into their own parents. If you saw them now, you'd never believe they were ever young. Who would name kids Summer and . . ." She stops talking.

"And what? What's your name?" I don't know why I asked her that. I don't care what her name is.

"My name is so dumb. I don't usually tell people."

"Tell me," I order.

She sighs. "It's Breezy. Summer and Breezy. Stupid names. But everybody just calls me Bree. I don't mind that."

"Bree? That's not a name either."

"I know, it's a cheese."

"It is?"

"So tell me your name now. I told you mine."

I get up and start walking around again. Does it matters if she knows my name? I don't know. I don't think I want to hear her say it, though.

"No," I say. "I don't have a name."

I keep thinking about what she said about her parents, how they used to be hippies but now they're old farts. "I know why they changed," I say.

"Who changed?"

"Your parents. I bet they got weird and scared after your sister died. I bet they were okay before that."

She shrugs. "Maybe. I don't remember."

"Believe me," I tell her, "that's what did it. When somebody dies, everybody else changes."

"Is that what happened in your family . . . when your sister . . ."

For a second I can almost see Michelle standing there—almost, but not quite. "I miss her." I didn't mean to say it out loud, but I guess I did.

"I'm sorry," the girl says. When I look at her, she's twisting her wrists around in the rope, which is going to give her a burn if she doesn't stop. "Listen. Can I just ask you, what's going on here?" she says. "I mean, if we're just sitting around, if you're not going to . . . do anything . . . I was supposed to be home a long time ago. My mother probably has the entire Massachusetts police force out looking for me, but if I go home right now, she'll call them off."

Just when I was starting to feel a little better about her, she says that. Like she's in charge here. Like I'm the one tied up and she's the one with the knife. Hah!

"Just because I haven't killed you yet doesn't mean

I'm not going to!" I tell her. "Maybe I should just do it right now and get it over with." I pick the knife up from where I threw it on the floor and hold it tight at her throat again.

"No, don't! I'm sorry! Please don't kill me! Please! People would miss me the same way you miss your sister!"

I never scared anybody this bad before. I can feel her shoulders trembling right through the coat. "How do you know about Michelle? I didn't tell you about her!"

"You . . . you told me she died. That's all. You didn't tell me any . . . details."

The muscles in her neck are tight and stringy; she's waiting for me to pull the knife across them like a violin bow. It makes me feel sick, how scared she is. It reminds me of sitting in the courtroom while those pictures flashed on the big screen. I was thirteen. I puked up my guts.

I put the knife down. "You think *I* killed her?"

She rubs her throat with her tied-together hands. The bandanna's all soaked with her crying. "I don't know. Did you?"

"No, I didn't. My mother says I did, but it was Novack. I never killed anybody."

"You haven't?"

"No. But I never stopped anybody from being killed either."

Leo

We're just sitting here. I tried to look through some of these magazines that are down here, just to get my mind off the situation I'm in, but the words didn't make sense, so I gave up. My head hurts too much to read anyway—like somebody's squeezing my brains. The girl, Bree, she's not gabbing anymore. She's slumped over with her head on the arm of the couch, but she's not asleep. She's not moving a muscle, but she's all tense. Probably pretending to be someplace else. Or trying to use E.S.P. to get a message to her mother. Trying to phone home like E.T.

I loved that movie. Our whole family watched it together back when we had a VCR. Back when we had a family.

My head hurts like it's about to crack open, and Michelle's not telling me what I'm supposed to do. The pictures are *still* flashing up in my brain, although not constantly now. Maybe they'll be there forever. Maybe killing this girl won't make them stop. What if it doesn't? What if she's not as bad as I thought at first, just dressed stupid?

If I had some clues about her, I'd know what to do next. Not just this stuff she's telling me: about her boyfriend, and her poor mother, and going to college. Not that shit. If I knew the stuff she hides from people, the bad stuff, then I'd know if she was the right one to kill or not. If she was the one who makes up for Michelle. But nobody tells anybody *that* stuff; you have to find it out some other way.

Michelle, tell me! What should I do?

I must have been talking out loud, because the girl sits up all of a sudden. "Who are you talking to? Is there somebody else down here or just ghosts?"

I look around, like I'm not sure myself. Ghosts. Michelle isn't a ghost. She's my . . . damn it. Where *is* she? I pick this big old wrench up off a shelf because it's the closest thing I see, and I let it fly against the wall. Makes an awful racket when it hits the concrete floor. I see the girl cowering on the sofa, like I might hit her next. But instead I just knock a bunch of books off a bookcase, which also makes a nice loud noise. But it doesn't change anything. I slump into a folding chair and try to stop my head from pounding.

After it's quiet for a minute, the girl sits up again and says, "It's ironic that my mother turns out to be right. All her silly worrying, and now she's actually right."

If Michelle won't talk to me, I'll have to talk to this girl, try to figure things out myself. "What's she right about?"

"Fenton is dangerous. You can't trust men. It's a rotten

world. All that paranoid mother stuff."

"Your mother says that? She's got one thing right: It *is* a rotten world. Fenton's not all that dangerous, though. You just have to know what parts are bad. You gotta be careful."

"Was she right about the not trusting men part?" she asks me.

She's got that bandanna on, and she's not even looking in my direction, but for some reason I feel like all of a sudden she can see me. "I don't know. My mother doesn't trust men either, but she's a Looney Tunes. My sister trusted a guy she shouldn't have and she's dead because of it. But I don't think most guys are like that. Most guys are okay."

"What about you? Are you okay?"

I don't know what to say. I used to be a guy you could trust, but this Bree girl doesn't know who I was before. She only knows the guy I am tonight. Whoever he is.

"I'm okay. Most of the time."

She snorts. "I just got lucky, I guess, being the girl who came along the one night you decide *not* to be okay, huh?" She's got this mouth once she gets going.

"You were asking for it with that outfit."

"What? I was not! I'm not the only girl who wears short skirts!"

"And a tight top and those shoes—out alone without a guy at night over by the bars . . ."

"Do you always have a girl along if you go out at night? Why shouldn't I be able to go someplace by myself if I want to? Why do I have to have a man along all the time?"

"Keep you safe."

"That's bull! All I was asking for was a beer and a game of pool. And if you think I wanted something else, you're wrong. I shouldn't have to have a bodyguard just to walk down a public street!"

She's all steamed up. One of those women's rights types. Funny thing is, I used to try to get Michelle to be more like that. Once she started going with Novack, she turned into his slave: did his shopping, cooked his dinner almost every night, cleaned up his pigsty place. I told her she was nuts to do all that. *Don't let him order you around,* I'd say. *Stand up for yourself!*

But she was afraid he'd leave her if he got mad. The bastard told her he had another girlfriend up in Maine and if Michelle didn't appreciate him, he'd go back to her. Only it turned out the one in Maine already had a restraining order out on him—we found that out at the trial—so she probably wasn't too anxious to start frying his hamburgers again.

Michelle was smart! She was a straight-A student with a scholarship to the state university. Why couldn't she tell Novack was a sick, lying psycho? It makes you think love is just a big blindfold you never want to put on.

"Gimme your purse," I say. And then I just grab it

from where it's been sitting there next to her all this time. It's one of those big sack things girls carry around that you wonder why they want to lug all that junk everywhere.

"If you wanted my money, you could have taken it hours ago. There's not that much anyway."

"I don't care about the money," I tell her. Although I get her wallet out first and check it. There's about forty bucks in there. Which is not much to her. Shit. Keep your stupid, rich-girl money. Four or five credit cards, a library card, a video rental card, her driver's license.

I look at the license picture. Funny, I don't even know what she looks like. Her face, I mean. I never looked at it and now it's mostly covered up. But the picture makes her look nice—brown eyes wide open and one of those silly driver's license smiles where you feel like a damn fool because all the other people waiting in line are watching you grin at nothing.

"You just had a birthday," I say.

"Last week. I'm eighteen." I'm still going through all her cards when she asks me, "How old are you?"

"About the same."

"You just had a birthday?"

"Not yet. Couple weeks."

"You mean I'm older than you?" She laughs.

"A few *weeks* older. Why is that so funny?"

She shrugs. "I guess it isn't. So happy birthday."

"Right." I flip to the photo section.

"Aren't you going to wish me a happy birthday?"

"You said it was last week."

"So? I wished you one and yours isn't for another two weeks."

I glare at her, but, of course, she doesn't even know it. "Happy goddamn birthday. How's that?"

"Thanks a million."

Man, my head hurts. It's like two lightning bolts slicing right into my eyes and coming out through the back of my skull. Making me feel sick. "You got any headache stuff in here?" I ask her.

"Yeah, there's some in that front pocket. You have a headache?"

Miss Sympathy. "Why else would I ask you?" I find the bottle and swallow two of them right down, then decide I might as well take a third one too. This is a bitch of a headache.

I go back to the wallet. She's got a few billion photographs stuffed in here. This one she's all dressed up, standing next to some guy with a rose in his lapel.

"Who's the bozo in the tux? Your boyfriend?"

"I guess. You're probably looking at our prom picture."

"Prom. What a waste of money. What's his name?"

"Jesse."

"You like him?"

"Of course I like him. I wouldn't go out with him if I didn't."

"He treat you good?"

"Better than you do."

"Yeah? Well, that's not saying much, is it? 'Cause I'm not exactly Prince Charming. Sorry to tell ya."

"Not tonight, anyway," she says.

Bree

All of a sudden he's really talking to me. He's going through the stuff in my purse and asking me questions. It's not that different from talking to any other guy, except that I'm tied up and blindfolded. Twice now he's held the knife up to me, but then he puts it down again; I don't think he really *wants* to hurt me. I wish I knew why I'm here. If he's not going to do anything, why did he grab me to begin with?

I can hear him pawing through my purse, pulling more stuff out. "What are you looking for?"

"Don't worry about it. I'm not taking anything. What's this list of names for? Jennifer Crawley, Bill DeLuca, Tony . . ."

"That's my list of who's working at the Main Meal next week. The volunteers. I have to make sure we have a full crew."

"These are all high school kids from Hawthorne?"

"Yeah. We go every other Monday night."

He snickers. "I guess it makes you all feel good about yourselves to hand out free slop to people who'll eat anything, and then go home and fix yourselves a big steak."

"We eat the same thing they do. When we're done serving. It's not slop."

"And *then* you pat yourself on the back and run on home."

"That's not how it is. I know I have things the people there probably never will, but I don't think I'm better than they are. Yeah, I guess I do feel good about it. But I'd rather feel good about serving somebody a free dinner than feel good about shopping at the mall."

"I work for my meals."

"Yeah," I say, "you're an upstanding citizen, all right." For some reason I feel like I can get away with a little bit of cheekiness now. Almost like I'm flirting.

"Now that I think of it, we did go in there once, just to check it out, when we were low on cash. But we didn't go back. We take care of ourselves."

"God knows, *you* don't need any help," I say. I'm really aggravated he wants me to feel bad about my work at the Main Meal—one of things I'm most proud of.

He's completely quiet for a minute. Then he says, "I thought you were afraid of me?"

I decide not to lie. "I am, but I'm trying not to act like it. It makes me feel better."

He grunts and goes back to rooting around in my

bag. "This note must be from your boyfriend. *I'll pick you up at 7:00. Wear that yellow sweater. Love, Jesse.*

What happens when you wear the yellow sweater?"

"He just likes it, that's all."

"Is it tight? Does it show you off?"

I don't like talking about this. "None of your business."

"Do you do what Jesse tells you? Did you wear the yellow sweater for him that night?" He doesn't sound like he's joking around, so I don't make a joke out of it either.

"No, I don't think I did. It's not my favorite. It's itchy."

He lets his breath out, long and slow. "That's good. That's good. He shouldn't boss you around."

I grunt. "That's what I tell him. He doesn't think he bosses me, but he does. He wants to make all the decisions. If it's *my* idea, chances are he won't like it."

"That's not good," he says immediately, like he's given this a lot of thought. "You don't need a guy telling you what to do all the time. You're a person too, aren't you?"

"Of course I am. I'm probably making Jesse sound worse than he is . . ."

"You should go to a different school."

"What?"

"Didn't you say he wanted you to go to the same college he does?"

"I didn't think you were *listening* to me."

"Go someplace else."

Well, okay, I feel like saying, I will if I get out of here alive! "What difference does it make to you?"

For a minute he doesn't say anything, and then he kind of explodes. "A girl should *never* let a guy run her life like that! You gotta make your own decisions! Goddammit, it's *your* life! Your *one life!*"

I have the feeling he's leaning over me, so I sit back a little. "Well, I know," I say. "I know it's my life."

"Good," he says. "Don't forget it." His footsteps back away.

Jesus, I'm lightheaded sitting here in the dark, having this absurd conversation. Who *is* this person? My stomach is growling now too, but maybe it's just angry. "I'm kind of hungry," I tell him. "Would you see if there's something in my purse? There's a secret zipper pocket down on one side where I keep some hard candy."

He looks, I guess, and finally finds it. "I didn't see that zipper before. It's hidden." I can hear him unwrapping the candy and my mouth starts to water. "How come girls always like to have secrets from guys? I never understood that."

His fingers touch my lips and I jump back, surprised, but then I realize he's holding a candy and trying to slip it into my mouth. I open up and let him gently slide it in. The sweet strawberry flavor is tinged with the salty taste of his fingers. "Thank you," I say. It tastes so good, like it's the first food I've had in weeks.

"If you're really hungry, I've got some crackers down here, and some root beer."

"You do? Could I have a root beer? I'm really thirsty."

"I'll get it." I can hear him walk across the room. A pop-top whooshes open. The wax paper crinkles on the cracker package. Pretty soon he sits down next to me, puts the soda can in my tied-together hands. "Can you hold this?"

"Yeah. Thanks." I tip the can and let the root beer slide down my throat. It's fabulous too, the best root beer I've ever had. Suddenly I have the odd feeling that I'm doing something I *want* to do. That I'm no longer being held here by force; I'm staying by choice. And even though I know it isn't really true, it makes me feel a little better.

"The crackers are right here, if you want one," he says. I hear him pick up my purse again and set it on his lap. I don't know what secrets he thinks he's going to uncover in there. A snotty tissue? A couple of Tampax? I don't have much of a secret life.

"You keep a pair of socks in your purse," he says. "How come?"

Well, there is *that* secret, isn't there? "Just so I have an extra pair, in case, you know, I need one."

"Why would you need extra socks?"

It's silly to be so embarrassed about this, but I always have been, ever since I was little. Mom used to make such a big deal about it.

"My feet get sweaty sometimes, and I need to change my socks." I never knew anybody else who had to do this.

"In school?"

"Sometimes. Like after gym. Or if I go to somebody's house after school and we take off our shoes."

"Why do you need clean socks every time you take off your shoes?"

I sigh. "If you must know, my feet sweat so badly that they stink. They just plain *stink* and I'm embarrassed to take my shoes off in front of people unless I run into the bathroom first and change my socks. So that's my big secret. I smell like a locker room."

For some reason I have the feeling he's staring at me. Then I hear him putting the stuff back in my purse. "Sweaty feet are no big deal. Stuff like that isn't important."

"It is to me."

"No, it isn't. Not really."

"How do you know? Maybe it wouldn't be to you, but it is to me."

"Well, then, it shouldn't be. If that's the only thing you're keeping secret, you're damn lucky."

I think about this a minute. "Maybe girls keep secrets from boys because it gives them a little bit of power. So boys don't know *everything,* the way they think they do."

"Girls can have all the power they want—they just have to take it, not wait for somebody to give it to them."

"You're the one who says girls aren't allowed to walk around in bad neighborhoods by themselves."

"I just meant for your own good, is all."

My own good? What is with this guy? One minute he's threatening me with a knife, and the next he's all concerned about my welfare. He gets up and I can hear him closing the cracker package, moving around.

"My mother always said me and Michelle were just alike when we were little—two peas in a pod. Both always begging to go to the swimming pool, or go out for Chinese food. We loved to play dress-up when we went to our gramma's house. And our favorite thing was going to the drive-in over in Mayfair before they closed it down; we'd play on the playground equipment in the dark with that big movie screen up over our heads. It was awesome. We liked all the same things."

"That's cool," I say quietly.

"That was when we were little. Before . . ."

We're both quiet. He sounds so normal now I'm thinking maybe he'll tell me the story of how she died, but he doesn't say anything else, and I'm afraid to ask him in case it makes him crazy again. Right now he seems almost . . . nice. I guess this sounds crazy, and I probably *am* getting crazy sitting here all night, but there's a way in which I almost like this guy.

"So how's your headache?" I say.

"It's a little better," he says. "Anyway, it's not killing me anymore. How's your lip?"

I put my hands up and touch it—it's puffy, but not that sore. "It's okay."

"I'm sorry," he says. "I never meant to hurt anybody."

I believe him.

12:45 A.M.

Bree

He's been quiet, but sort of restless. It sounded like he was walking around in circles for a while there, and then I heard a toilet flush. Which made me want to scream. I've got to pee so badly my ovaries are doing the backstroke, but I'm afraid to say anything. He'd probably have to go with me, since I'm all tied up and everything, and it just seems too horrible, not to mention dangerous, to pull down my panty hose in front of a guy who's more or less bonkers.

I don't think he's going to kill me or he'd have done it already. And I believe him that he doesn't really want to hurt me, but what he *does* have in mind is anybody's guess. Half the time he seems harmless, but then suddenly he gets crazy again. There must be some way to make him let me go. Advice for the future: Never drink a soda if you're tied up in a basement with a nut.

"Umm, hello? . . . Is there a bathroom here?" I finally have to ask him. There's no choice. It's gotten to the point where I feel like I can taste it in the back of my mouth, like my plumbing's backing up.

He doesn't say anything for a minute, but then: "You need it?"

"Yeah. I really do. Could you . . . show me?"

"Okay." He comes over and takes my arm to help me stand up; it's hard to balance yourself when your feet and hands are tied together. Oh, God, just standing is awful. It feels like there's a water balloon between my legs. "How far is it?" I whine.

"Not far."

I shuffle along and he guides me, holding me by the elbow, gently. My shoulder brushes a doorframe, so I guess this is it. Now what?

"It's right behind you. I'm not looking," he says. "Go ahead."

Maybe he is, maybe he isn't, but I'm glad anyway he *says* he isn't. I can't help it, though, I'm whimpering. It's impossible to get your clothes off with your hands and feet tied together. How can this be happening to me? I want to go *home*!

I manage to get my tights pushed down to my knees, but I can feel that I'm going to lose it before I get the job done, lose it in all possible ways.

Just then I feel him touch me, a rough hand on my hands, and I sob. Just once. Something will happen now.

"Don't worry. I'm just untying your hands so you can use them. That's all I'm doing." I feel the rope loosen and the tears start to gush. Just in time, I push my underwear down and manage to find the seat. All interior liquids pour out.

"You don't have to cry. I'm not looking at you." He

sounds scared, like an entirely different guy than the one who held the knife to my throat.

It's so humiliating, peeing blindfolded in some cellar with my feet tied together—I can't stop crying. Not to mention there's this strange guy standing in the room who *has* threatened to kill me. My wrists hurt too. The whole thing. I just slump over on the toilet and weep.

"Please," he begs me. "I put a roll of toilet paper by your shoe."

I reach down for it, a familiar object here in the Twilight Zone. I use it to mop up both ends of me, but don't dare to lift up the blindfold enough to see anything. I get shakily to my feet, reach down and pull up my underpants, my tights, smooth down my skirt.

"I'm finished," I say.

He takes my arm again. "There's no place to wash your hands down here. I'm sorry."

"Washing my hands is the least of my problems, isn't it?" I say, still sniffing. He doesn't answer.

I try to hold on to my crankiness to control the panic that came back with the tears. "Are you going to tie me up again? My wrists are sore."

"I don't want you to take off the blindfold."

"I won't. I promise."

"I don't want you to see me."

"Believe me, I don't want to see you."

He grunts. I guess this means okay. He leads me

back to the couch and gives me a little push back into it. What a relief. I peed, he took the rope off my wrists, I'm back on my couch. Things could be worse.

Leo

Jesus Christ, why am I doing this? This is just some girl I'm scaring the shit out of, a high school girl in a short skirt and smelly socks! Somebody who's afraid I'll see her take a piss! Not some slut who deserves fifty-seven stab wounds. How did I get so mixed up about this? I thought Michelle wanted me to . . . no, it's Ma's fault—she got me going with those goddamn pictures. Which are still upstairs. Waiting for me.

Stop thinking about the pictures! That's how this got started to begin with. And it isn't really Ma's fault either. It's *his* fault. Fucking Novack. He's the one that really started it all. Finished it all. Finished us all off.

Bree interrupts my thoughts. "Listen, if we're going to stay up all night, how about telling me a story or something? To take my mind off things."

I don't know what she's talking about. "A story? What?"

"You know. A story. About you or somebody you know. Or one you heard. Or make one up. Just for something to do."

I shake my head, but she can't see me. "I can't make up stories. I'm no good at that stuff."

"Well, tell me the truth then." Her voice is stiff and she's still rubbing the bruised places on her wrists where the rope was tied. I hurt her.

"The truth would be worse than something I made up."

She sighs. "Okay. I'll tell you a story then."

"Go ahead," I say. "Since you love to talk so much." God, she goes from crying to storytelling in two minutes. I never met anybody like this.

"Let's see. Okay, a story." She takes a deep breath. "When I was a little kid, my grandmother lived with us. My mother's mother. And she took care of me all the time because my mother was going to law school and she was too busy. I really adored her, my grandmother. At least that's what my mother says. I don't remember too much about her anymore."

"She died?"

"I'm getting to that part. She got sick when I was four years old and died just a few weeks before I was supposed to start kindergarten. I don't remember this either, but my mother tells me I'd have a stomachache every single morning and refuse to go to school. If they made me go, I'd throw up all over the doorstep of the building. I guess because I was afraid to leave home or something. Who knows? Anyway, Summer was born by then, so my mother had more than she could handle with the two of us and no help. So that was the end of law school."

She stops talking and starts pulling on strands of her hair and wrapping them around her fingers. "Is that it?" I ask.

"That would be a pretty lame ending, wouldn't it? No, here's the real story: One night after she'd died—I don't know how long after—she came and sat on my bed in the middle of the night."

"You dreamed it."

"Maybe. But the thing is, this couldn't have been something my mother told me about, because she wasn't there, and I'm sure if I told her at the time, she'd have said the same thing you just did. It wouldn't have been important to her. But it was important to me, because I believed it. I saw her in her saggy black dress and her neat white bun, and I'll never forget it. Even though she didn't actually say anything, I knew she'd come back to tell me not to be afraid. And after that I wasn't. I could go to school and everything. Because I knew she was still around. Somewhere."

"You really believe that?" I ask her. I've been thinking she's smarter than this.

"I believe I believed it. That's enough."

"A kid believes that kind of thing—grown-ups don't. People don't come back for a visit. When they die, they're gone. This I know."

"Michelle talks to you, doesn't she? And she's dead."

I feel dizzy for a minute. I forgot about her for a while there. I forgot about Michelle! How could I *ever* . . . "She doesn't come back, though. I don't *see* her."

She shrugs. "You talk to her. What's the difference?"

"Big difference. Besides, I don't . . . I don't really believe . . ." Was it true? Yes. "I don't really believe I was talking to her. It was just . . . in my head."

She nods in agreement. "In my experience, they don't talk."

I don't answer, but I smile at her, which, of course, she can't see. "You're a good storyteller. I'm glad I picked you."

She grunts. "Next time get a library book."

1:30 A.M.

Leo

HERMIT FARMER LEAVES FORTUNE TO HOMETOWN LIBRARY was the headline that caught my attention. There were a bunch of old newspapers in a pile on one of the shelves, so I figured I'd read her a story. Better than telling her stuff about my crappy life.

Hugo Elsworth Vorhees, who had lived alone on a small, run-down farm for the past fifty-eight years, left more than a million dollars to the McAlister County Library in Vida Lake, Iowa, when he died last month at age eighty-nine. Vorhees's handwritten will was found in a safe deposit box in a local bank along with a number of stock certificates.

Local residents were shocked. "Hugo never acted like he had a dime," said grocery store owner Victor Yoder. "When he came in here, he just bought the basics. Bread and coffee and stuff. Hardly ever even bought a newspaper." As far as most people knew, Vorhees's only income came from fixing clocks and other small appliances people brought to his farm. He owned a thirty-year-old truck, but seldom drove it the three miles into town.

Most amazed of all was Sandra Wheeler, librar-

ian of the one-room McAlister County Library. "As far as I know, Hugo Vorhees never stepped foot in here. I'm not sure he could even read," said Wheeler. The librarian, though very grateful for the bequest, also said, "I just don't know what we're going to do with a million dollars' worth of books about our feline friends."

Vorhees's will specifies that the money be used to purchase books on the subject of cats. Friends told reporters Vorhees always fed the strays that came to his barn, but never let a cat into his house.

"Man, that's the craziest thing I ever heard of." I look over at Bree, who's got her head laid back against the old sofa. "Don't you think?"

She rolls her head toward me. "Well, it's strange, I guess. Not the strangest thing I ever heard of, though." She sounds tired now, like she can hardly make herself talk.

"You mean, like, tonight is stranger?"

"It's pretty high on *my* list," she says. I'm starting to like the way she talks, kind of smartass, but *true*. I don't know exactly what I mean by that. Maybe that I believe the things she says. She's not full of bull.

"If you had a lot of money, and you knew you were going to die, who would you leave it to?"

"Why? I'm not going to die, am I?"

I'm not even thinking of that right now. But I guess

I can see why she would be. I don't want to tell her anything for sure yet, though. I just want to talk to her. "I don't know," I say. "I have to figure some things out."

"Well, I wish you'd figure them out already. I'm exhausted. Aren't you?"

"Listen, I asked you a question. Who would you leave your money to?"

She gives an enormous sigh, which still has a little fear in it. I'm sorry for that, so I speak quietly. "I just want to talk a little," I say. "You like to talk."

She sits up and rotates her head back and forth between her shoulders a few times like you see on those exercise shows. "Okay. If I had piles of money, who would I leave it to . . . ? A charity, I guess. Maybe I'd give it to the Main Meal or something. I don't know."

"You would? You wouldn't give it to a person? You could make somebody so happy!"

She shrugs. "Maybe. Maybe not. You know how when people win the lottery it always ruins their lives. I wouldn't want that to happen."

"I never heard that, that people's lives got ruined by getting rich."

"Sure, it happens all the time. Their friends and relatives suddenly buddy up to them and want some money, and then get jealous and mad because they don't think they got enough. The people quit their jobs, but then they're bored and don't know what to do with themselves. All their friends are still working and can't afford to take big vacations with them or anything. They start feeling guilty about the money. It's terrible."

I guess it could happen that way. I always thought money would save you from craziness, not sink you in deeper. "So you'd give it to the Main Meal, huh?"

"Maybe. That way it would help a lot of people."

"Who can't help themselves."

"Sometimes people need help, for God's sake! There's nothing wrong with asking for it. You're so judgmental. We've had people who used to be guests, but once they start doing better financially, they come back and help other people. Why let yourself just fall apart if there are people who can help you? Get yourself back together and then you can help somebody else!"

I'd been thinking about who I'd give my millions of dollars to, probably Gramma, if she was still alive when I got it, or Aunt Suzanne, or maybe Ronnie at the garage. He'd be stoked. Or I could buy a million dollars' worth of library books that would warn girls not to go with guys like Novack. But then Bree got all excited, and it was hard not to pay attention to her when she talked like that, so damned sure of herself.

"You mean me?" I asked her. "You saying I should get help?"

"It couldn't hurt, could it?"

I almost laughed at that. "Of course it could hurt. Everything hurts. You don't know."

"I don't know if you don't tell me."

"Believe me, you do not want to hear what I could tell you," I say, and I start flipping through magazines again, though I can't tell what I'm looking at. I pretend my heart isn't banging so hard it's making me feel sick. For some reason, I *want* to tell her. I can feel the words lining up in my throat and I keep swallowing them back down. I *can't* let them out.

She shifts around on the couch so she's facing me, like she's really trying to see through the blindfold. "I do want you to tell me. What else can we do? We're alone in some basement. You aren't hurting me, but you aren't letting me go either. I mean, maybe this whole evening isn't so strange, maybe you brought me here because you needed to tell somebody the whole story. It can't hurt . . ."

"Yes, it goddamn well can!" I scream at her. I throw a couple of magazines across the room and slam my foot against the cement floor. "It hurts *me*!" Jesus Christ, I think I'm crying.

2:45 A.M.

Bree

He told me the story. It took him a few minutes to get started on it—first he just threw things around and sort of screamed and cried at the same time. I thought maybe I'd really pushed him too far, but I almost didn't care. At least *something* was happening.

Once he started talking, it seemed like I was sitting there listening to his thick voice for hours, but it couldn't have been that long. He was so mad when he started, yelling that somebody named Novack had murdered his older sister four years ago today. Slit her throat and stabbed her fifty-seven times. He kept repeating that, like the number fifty-seven had some special meaning.

After a while he was hardly even talking to me, just talking, just getting the story out. Over and over he said he should have stopped her from going to Novack's house that night. I didn't say anything. It was such a horrible story there was nothing I *could* say. I think if I'd heard it from my mother, sitting in our comfy living room, I'd have said, "Please, Mom, spare me the details!" Even though I'd only be half-listening anyway, the way I usually do with her. But for some weird reason, sitting in a basement with a guy who'd threatened to *kill* me, I wanted to hear it all. I wanted to know what makes a person go over the edge. I guess it was the answer to *Why am I here?*

He told me about sitting in the courtroom and seeing bloody photographs of his sister projected onto a huge screen. I imagined the pictures on the black screen of my eyes, but couldn't imagine *really* seeing them. He told me how his mother had lost her daughter, then her job, her husband, and, finally, her mind. And then he told me what had happened upstairs earlier this evening, which made the hair stand up on my arms.

He's quiet for several minutes before I dare to speak. "No wonder," I say, and everything really does make sense now.

"So now you know," he says. "I really am a psycho."

"Novack's the psycho," I say. "You and your mother, you're his victims."

"Michelle was the victim," he says, but he's not fiery anymore. Telling the story has quieted him down. He sounds collapsed, like a flat tire.

"She was, but so are you." He doesn't say anything. I don't hear a sound.

"I'm glad you told me," I say, and I hear him choke out a scoffing noise.

"Right. It's as good as a Stephen King novel."

"That's not what I mean. It was hard to listen to, but I'm glad you . . . I don't know . . . trusted me."

Again, no answer.

"So is your mother . . . is she still upstairs?" I wasn't

just curious—I wanted to know where all the characters were located.

"She has to be. She never goes out. What kind of shape she's in, I don't know."

"And the . . . pictures?"

I can hear him get up and pace around a little. "Yeah, I guess they're still up there too. I'm done talking about this now, okay? I can't talk about it anymore. I can't think about it. I can't *deal* with it . . ." His teeth sound as chattery as mine were when I first got here.

"Okay. We don't have to talk about it anymore. Are you cold? You want your coat back?"

"No, I'm fine. I just can't talk anymore. I'm not used to it, you know?" He's pacing around again.

"Sure," I say, though I don't really know. "We can talk about something else if you want."

"No! I mean, no. I'm sorry, but I just have to stop thinking. Okay? I just need to be quiet."

"Okay." Quiet I can understand. Quiet is fine. Although I do wish there was something I could say to help him. I know *somebody* could help him; he's just mixed up, not terrible or anything. And I wish I could lift up the bandanna for just a second, to see what he looks like. But I don't dare.

"Let's just . . . look, there's this old TV down here," he says. "I forgot about it. The reception sucks and it's just black and white, but . . ."

"I can't see it anyway," I remind him.

"Yeah. Right." He gives a little sort of laugh. "I'll plug it in over here and see what's on. Sometimes late at night there's crazy stuff . . . just to clear my head, you know? Forget about things. I can't just keep talking . . . It's too much." He's scooting something across the floor—if that's the TV, it's heavy.

"That sounds good," I say. Whatever he needs is fine with me. Nobody should have to live through things like that. Nobody should have a night like tonight.

Leo

I don't know why I told her the whole story like that. I never told anybody before. Even the people who already know about it—we don't discuss it. In four years, I only ever talked about it to myself.

She was okay, though. She just listened. I don't think she blamed me. She didn't blame me.

I shove the big old TV set around so it's in front of the couch and plug it in. We won't be able to get much on it this late—there's no cable hookup or anything. I flip through the stations—news, movie, talk show, another movie. It doesn't really matter. I just have to stop thinking.

"Here's a Sherlock Holmes movie, it looks like. Is that okay? It's in black and white anyway."

"That's fine," she says. "It sounds kind of buzzy."

I play around with the knobs and get it a little better, but not much. "Best I can do," I say. I turn to look at her and she looks ridiculous staring at a TV set with a blindfold over her eyes. "I'm sorry you can't see it," I tell her.

It looks like she's smiling at me, but with the triangle of the handkerchief falling over her mouth, I can't be sure. "That's okay," she says.

"Would it be all right . . . would you mind if I sat next to you? So I can see the TV better?"

Her body gets kind of tight. "I guess you can." She scoots over closer to the arm rest and leans on it a little. It's not one of those really long sofas—more like a two-seater, so I'm kind of close to her, but I try not to touch her. I'm done with scaring her—I hate that I did that.

It's hard to hear the movie, but I don't care what they're saying anyway. She probably doesn't either. We're just waiting. Waiting for this night to be over.

4:30 A.M.

Bree

I wake up gradually, aware of a weight against my shoulder and a buzzing sound like a swarm of mellow flies congregating nearby. I've been dreaming that my mother is pregnant, which is pretty ridiculous for a fifty-year-old anyway, but then she gets her belly button pierced too. I'm thinking: Typical weird dream. But when I try to open my eyes and can't, it all floods back to me: where I am, how I got here, who I'm with.

I panic for a minute and sit up straight, which makes the weight on my shoulder shift too, and grunt a little, before the hollow breathing of a deep sleeper begins again. Who else could it be but my favorite kidnapper?

The boy who never sleeps is conked out on my shoulder while the TV white noise hums. His weight is against my left side, which prickles and pulses as if it's more alive than the rest of me. The obvious thought rushes through my mind: Can I possibly get out of here without waking him up? But it doesn't seem likely. I'd have to bend over to untie my ankles and his head would flop down on the couch. He'd feel me getting up. Even if I chucked these dumb shoes, I couldn't outrun him barefooted.

The panic subsides. He hasn't hurt me so far, not

since the bloody lip episode anyway, and I don't think he will. Besides, this whole thing isn't exactly his fault. I remember the story he finally told me, how quiet he became once he'd said it all out loud. I guess that was when he became real to me too. I know it sounds nuts, but I sort of *like* feeling him asleep next to me, his weight resting against me. As if I could be healing him somehow.

Boy, would that idea make my mother nuts. I can just hear her: "Is that what they teach you down at that soup kitchen? That it's up to you to save every Needy Ned that comes along?" She's not as horrible as I make her sound, just scared of so many things. Murderers, rapists, kidnappers. And since you can't always tell right off who might be one, to be on the safe side, you might as well just be afraid of everybody.

But if you're afraid, you're paralyzed. And even though I'm still here in the basement with my ankles tied together, I'm not afraid anymore. I think things are going to be okay. Carefully I move my right hand up and peel back the blindfold. I have to blink my eyes to get them to focus. At first I can hardly tell what I'm looking at—it's been so long since I've seen anything—but then I calm down. It's dark, except for an overhead bulb in a far corner and the gray light from the snowy television. The walls are stone, my couch is brown, there are cobwebs in the corners. Just a basement, like I thought. *My* basement, is what I'm thinking. The basement I'll never forget. I'm glad to see the big wooden shelves full of magazines and dishes, a toolbox, cookie tins, cans of paint, old shoes. This is a home. This is his home.

I know I'm going to look at him too. I want to, and I don't want to. If I don't, I'll always wish I had. But when I do, I can't see much anyway; he's too close to me. His face is pointed down toward my lap and all I can really see is the back of his head and one ear tucked tightly against his scalp. He's wearing a green sweatshirt, but if it has a name or anything on it, I can't see. His hair is brown, a little bit curly, long in the neck, in need of a trim. Like a hundred other guys I could name. No other identifying marks. Just a boy, like I thought.

There's nothing else to see, and I don't want him to know I peeked, so I slide the blindfold back down over my eyes and nose, feeling more comfortable in this darkness than I would have imagined I could a few hours ago. What, I wonder, would Caitlin say if she knew? If I could call her up right now and explain where I was and why I couldn't come home quite yet? Caitlin has no patience with any sort of adventure—it's hell on a manicure. She'd say something like "You can be so aggravating, Bree."

And Jesse. Angry, definitely angry. "I *told* you not to go to Fenton. How could you go when I told you *not* to?" Maybe *because* you told me not to—did you ever think of that? If only Jesse listened to me once in a while. I mean, really, when your *kidnapper* listens to you better than your *boyfriend* does, the relationship is probably headed for the Dumpster. Just because Jesse's so sure he's right about everything, does that necessarily mean I'm wrong about everything? The more I think about it, I don't see Jesse and me making it in the long run. I'm not interested in one of those marriages where two people just tolerate each other for twenty-five years because by that time nobody else will.

Which brings me to my parents . . . I keep trying to imagine what they've been doing all night tonight, and whether they've been doing it together or in separate rooms. What small conversations they've been forced to have with each other:

"Shall I call the police?" (she says)

"If you think it's necessary." (he says)

"Yes, I do. Don't you?" (she)

"You know her better than I do." (he)

"Well, you're her father!" (she)

"But you're her mother." (he)

"Where could she be?" (she)

"How on earth should I know?" (he, much annoyed with the whole affair)

Which would be the longest talk they've had in about ten years. I wonder if my friend here is right—that it started when Summer died. It never occurred to me because I don't really remember too much about that. I was still getting over Grandma's death, and Summer was just a little kid pain-in-the-neck to me anyway. Maybe

I'd be crazy about her by now, but at the time I don't think the loss affected me too much. I can see that if your child fell off a wall and died while you were both just standing there, it might make things weird for the parents. Like whose fault was it? The kid's fault? The mother's? The father's? Nobody's?

You know everybody around you is asking themselves that question; everybody wants to pin the blame somewhere. Even people you don't know who read about it in the newspaper. I've done it too. BOY HIT BY CAR. How did that happen? Did he run out in front of the car? Wasn't the driver paying attention? And where was that kid's mother anyway? If you can find somebody to blame, it makes you feel safer. It wasn't just some random, terrible event that could happen to anybody; it was someone's *fault*.

And who's fault is it that I'm not home in bed right now? I wonder if that point has been debated yet. God. Mom didn't want me to go, but she couldn't stop me. I hope she knows that. I was *going*. Well, it'll be all right anyway, because I'm not going to die. Not now. He gave me candy from my purse. He took me to the bathroom. He read me the newspaper article about the guy who gave his life savings to cat lovers. He's crazy, I guess, but he's not a killer.

How about those pictures upstairs? Let's put the blame on those, the grotesque photographs his mother keeps to drive herself batty. I wish I could get rid of them somehow. I think he'd be okay if I could get rid of the pictures. That's the thing to do, but how?

Without really thinking about it, my hand reaches over and touches his head. I pet him lightly, like you do a child, or a small animal, as if to say, *Don't worry*. I like the feeling, his hair under my fingers. But after a few strokes, he shudders, then wakes up. I'm sorry about that.

He pulls away from me, sits up. "What . . . what are you doing?"

"I don't know. Just sitting here with you."

He's disoriented. "I was sleeping. God, I was *sleeping*, wasn't I?"

"Yeah."

He gets up. "Why didn't you run away, for God's sake?" His voice has a cracking sound to it, as if he's upset.

"I don't know. It seemed too hard."

"Jesus, you should have gotten the hell out of here! I tied you up! I hurt you!"

"Not that much," I say, but I'm starting to feel like a fool, defending myself for sticking around.

"You weren't touching me, were you?" he asks. "I must have dreamed that."

I'm tired of answering questions that make me feel silly. "Listen," I tell him. "I've been thinking. We need to come up with a plan."

Leo

I was dreaming about my mother. She was happy, like she used to be, playing her old Rolling Stones records and dancing around. She smiled at me and stroked my head like she did when I was little. It was really nice, but all of a sudden I woke up and the person stroking me wasn't my mother. At first I couldn't figure out who it was, but then I remembered the girl. Bree. I brought her here all tied up. I had the knife. One minute a dream—the next minute a nightmare I can't wake up from.

I can't believe I really fell asleep. I was so tired after I told her, Bree, the story. She *wanted* me to tell it, and once I got started, I couldn't stop. I told her all of it, about the police coming to the door, about Ma screaming for three days, about the courtroom and the photographs and Gramma's knife. She just listened. When I couldn't talk anymore, I turned on the TV and I guess I must have fallen asleep. And then, while I was sleeping, instead of running away, she came up with this idea.

"We have to get rid of the pictures," she says. "So you never have to see them again. So your mother never sees them again."

I shake my head. "I'll never see them again because I'm never going up there again. I'm leaving here for good. Today."

"You can't just leave," she says.

I don't know what to say, so I stand up and walk around the room a little bit. I'm confused by the whole thing. "Why can't I leave? Why didn't *you* leave?"

She shrugs. "My legs are still tied. And I don't know where I am."

"Right." I bend down and untie her ankles. "Is that better? I'm sorry. I don't know what to say to you . . . about all of this."

She bends over and rubs her ankles, takes off her shoes. "Yeah. Thanks." I can see by looking that her feet have sweated through the heavy tights. A doggy kind of odor comes drifting up. "Oh, God," she says. "Now you know I wasn't lying."

"It's not so bad," I tell her. It's not; I mean that.

"Now who's lying?" she says.

I'm starting to sweat myself, remembering everything I did last night. "Listen, are you going to call the police? I mean, I know you'll have to . . ."

"I don't know who you are," she says. "What could I tell them? I don't even know where I am."

I have no right to ask her for anything, but I do. "Would you mind . . . would you keep the blindfold on until I drive you somewhere safe? As soon as it gets light out I'll take you to the diner. They open at six o'clock. You can call somebody from there. But I don't want you to see me."

"That's fine. I don't want to see you either."

"You don't?"

"If they ask me questions . . . I won't know anything."

"You know some things."

She shakes her head. "I don't think so." She's really smiling now—I'm sure of it.

"You're a strange person," I tell her.

"I'm strange?" she says, laughing.

I wish I could take off the blindfold and see her.

5:15 A.M.

Leo

Her plan is we go upstairs and get the photographs. I'll have to pick them up, of course, since she can't see, but I'll hand them to her upside down so I don't look at them any more than absolutely necessary. Since she can't see anyway, they won't bother her. Then we get rid of them someplace; she thought maybe a Dumpster.

At first I said no, I wasn't going back up there for anything. And I certainly wasn't taking her with me.

"She's your mother," Bree says. "She's all screwed up."

"She's all screwed up. Look at me!"

"This is your chance to get rid of them once and for all. Then she won't be able to look at them again either. Maybe she'll even get well."

"Miracles don't happen," I tell her. But I'm starting to think it isn't such a terrible idea. The damn things should have been destroyed years ago anyway. *Nobody* should ever have to look at them again. Of course, it means walking into hell to get them. Who knows what Ma's done up there? What if there's something even worse to look at by now? I can think of a thousand what-ifs.

"Why take chances, Bree? Why not just sit here

until it gets light and let me take you to the diner? It's too risky for you to go up there. I might get crazy again."

She thinks a minute. "I'm not afraid of you anymore. You called me Bree."

There's no way to go directly from the basement to our apartment, so we go around the house and in the front door. It's starting to get light out and I'm worried somebody will see us, me leading a girl with a rag tied over her eyes. What would they think? What if they call the police? But I don't have many choices now. Bree will probably call the police anyway, once she's safe at home and thinks it all over.

She stumbles going up the steps and I put my arm around her waist to steady her; she doesn't flinch or anything, but I let go right away anyhow. It's nice to touch someone like that. I never get to do it. I think about how if Michelle was alive, I'd be taller than her now. I could lean down and put my arm around her waist this same way—I could take care of her.

"Let me go in by myself first," I say. "Just to see where she is. Just in case . . ." I don't explain in case of what. Bree stands in the doorway while I sneak into the living room. No blood, no vomit, no sign of Ma except for an ashtray full of butts. I glance into the dining room on my way to her bedroom, and there she is, sitting in a dining room chair, head and arms sprawled across the table, a bottle of vodka knocked over sideways, ruining the finish on Gramma's oak table.

I can hear the snoring from here, so she's not dead. Thank God, thank God. I realize I've been holding my breath and I let it out. I hope Ma's had enough booze to be good and passed out; I don't want her to see Bree, or vice versa. God knows what would happen. Before I go back for Bree, I look at Ma and try to remember when she was a regular person and not a total wreck. When she got up early, took a shower, combed her hair, fixed us all lunches, and went off to work. When she smiled at me and knew who I was. It's been a long time. I'm glad Bree can't see her, can't see any of this.

I take Bree's arm and lead her into the kitchen. "We have to be quiet," I whisper. "My ma's sleeping in the next room." And then I glance quickly around the kitchen, close my eyes and start to shake.

"Are they in here?" she whispers.

"I can't make myself look yet," I say. I'm pinching my eyes closed so hard, they hurt. I can't open them. I can't.

"If I could take this off a minute, I could just get them . . ."

"No! I don't want you to! Please!" I'm talking too loud—I know that, but I can't have her seeing these things. I can't!

From the other room I hear moaning, shifting, swearing. "Damn it. Who the hell . . . ? Somebody in there?"

Without thinking, I clap a hand over Bree's mouth,

though I'm the one who spoke too loud, woke the witch. She sneaks an inch or two closer to me, as if she's hiding. I take my hand from her mouth and put it around her shoulder. We stand like stones, like statues, frozen in position, waiting for somebody to swing a magic wand over us and say, "You're free!"

The muttering from the other room continues, but gets slower. I'm hoping she's too drunk to get up and walk around. She says, "Nobody gives a shit, do they?" Then, lower, more slurred: "Bring me a drink." The rest is too muddy to understand. For a minute there's no sound, then the clunk of the empty vodka bottle hitting the rug. Will she get up now to search for more booze?

We wait. I think I can feel Bree's heart beating, but probably it's my own. Minutes pass and there are no more sounds from the dining room. I let my hand pass slowly across Bree's back—which shivers—as I turn to peek around the corner. Asleep again, head turned sideways, breathing deep. Thank you, Ma.

"It's okay." I whisper right into Bree's ear. And then there's nothing left to do but open my eyes and look, so I do. They're still here, strewn around the floor and countertops, just the way we left them.

"They're here," I say, trying to look through slitted eyes, so I can't make out any details.

"Do it fast," Bree orders. "Pick them up, turn them over, hand them to me. Fast!"

I do what she says, moving quickly around the

room. Pick it up, turn it over, give it to Bree. I get a glimpse of a shoulder, long brown hair, my poor dead sister—but I turn it over and keep going. Pick it up, turn it over, give it to Bree. Pick it up, turn it over, give it to Bree. I'm a machine, working well. I have a job to do and I'm doing it. Pick it up, turn it over, give it to Bree. When I hand her the last one, she turns the stack so she's cradling Michelle against her chest. I'm crying so quietly even God can't hear me.

I take Bree's arm and lead her back out through the living room. We run so lightly it feels like dancing. I don't look over at Ma in case she has the power to freeze me up again. I open the door and we glide down the front stairs.

It's really light out now; there are people outside, picking up their newspapers, getting into cars, but no one looks at us. A boy leading a blindfolded girl—they'd think it was just a prank of some kind. If she screamed, would they help her? Would they pretend not to hear? Or are they heroes? You can't tell by looking. I think most people are too busy to imagine anyone else's life; they just want to get on with their own. Or maybe it's just too early in the morning for heroes.

Once we're in the alley, it's darker again; the sun isn't high enough yet to light up this ugly place. I'm not sure it's ever that high.

"Is this where the Dumpster is?" Bree asks.

"Yeah, but I have another idea," I say. "I want to

burn them. So they'll never come back. So nobody else will ever see them either."

She nods her head. "Is there a place here to do it?"

"You're not supposed to, but our building super sometimes burns stuff in this old oil can back here. If we do it fast, we won't get caught." I get out my lighter. "I guess I'll take them now," I say.

But when I try to pull them from her hands, she holds on tight. "No, let me hold them. You shouldn't. Just tell me where the can is, and when to let them go," she says.

I position her hands over the oil can, my sister upside down and ready to disappear again, this time for good. It is for good, I tell myself. It's the best thing. This isn't the real Michelle anyway. The real Michelle is buried under a flat gray stone in Fenton Woods Cemetery. Or maybe the real Michelle is still in my mind. Maybe if I burn these terrible pictures, she'll come back some night, just the way she was, and sit on my bed.

I set the lighter at the edge of the stack and flick it. Orange flames immediately begin to eat up the slick paper.

"Now!" I say. "Let go!"

She does, and the pile falls in a fiery chunk to the bottom of the can. When I look in, the flames are already finishing up the job, turning paper to ash. Bree has stepped back. She closes her hands together like a child making a church and steeple with her fingers. I look at her hands and I think maybe I was wrong. Maybe there are miracles; maybe it's not too early in the morning for heroes.

Bree

It's not all that cold out but I'm shivering like crazy, even though I'm still wearing his coat. I think I feel so shaky now because it's over but it's not over. I'm in the dark, tiptoeing around an apartment where a crazy woman lives, I'm standing in an alley with her sometimes-berserk son who I'm now befriending, helping him burn photos of his murdered sister. I think what's really scary this morning is that I'm not sure who I am now, or who I'll be when this is over, when I'm back at home, safe.

Am *I* crazy? Maybe. But I think I'm doing the right things. I'm doing what I have to do. Not just to live. Not just to get out of here. But to get out of here *well*.

After we burn the pictures, he's quiet for a long time. I feel like I'm at a funeral. I even pray a little bit, which I almost never do. I say, *Dear God, whoever you are, help us get through this. Help all our mothers and fathers and friends. And tell our poor dead sisters we miss them.*

6:30 A.M.

Leo

I drive using both hands this time. Bree slumps down in the seat without me even telling her to. It's light enough now for people to notice the blindfold, but they won't the way she has one arm across her face. I wish I was taking her out to breakfast and then driving her home, like we were normal people. I stop down the block from the diner, which already has a bunch of cars and trucks parked outside.

"The cops have probably found your car by now," I tell her. She nods, and I can't think of what else to say. "The diner's a nice place. There's a phone—you can call your parents. Or the police. Or whoever."

"Thanks," she says, but she doesn't leap right out of the car, and I'm glad.

"Don't be thanking me," I say. "God. I'm so sorry about this whole thing."

"Are you really leaving Fenton?" she asks.

"I don't know. I have to think. I don't know what to do."

She's quiet for a minute. "Could you . . . let me know?"

"Bree, how can I do that?"

"Right," she says, then slips my coat off her shoulders. "You better take this back. Do you want your handkerchief? I'll close my eyes."

I do want it—it seems like part of her now. "Yeah," I say, and gently untie the knot, letting my fingers scoop through her hair a little, just a touch. She takes a deep breath, then puts her fingers to her eyes and massages them.

"Are you okay?"

"Yeah." She puts one hand on the door handle.

"Wait!" I say. She'll be gone. In just another moment. Gone forever.

She freezes. Scared again? I don't want that.

"I . . . I just wanted to say, happy birthday, Bree."

She laughs quietly, which I love. "Happy birthday to you too . . . whoever you are," she says.

Before I can think it over too much, I lean in close to her shoulder and whisper, "Leo. My name is Leo."

"Leo," she repeats. "Thank you for telling me, Leo." Then she opens the door and gets out, stands on the sidewalk with her back to the car. Her beautiful rich-girl hair shines in the sun.

I squeal away from the curb fast, in case she turns around, in case I *wait* for her to turn around. I don't know where I'm going, only that I'm going away from her.

Bree

I can hardly bear to open my eyes. It's too sunny, too bright, too real. I stand here for a minute, blinking, rubbing my eyes, but nobody pays any attention. The diner is just down the street; two guys with paint-spattered pants are going in the glass door. I look around, even though I heard the car speed away, and then I go inside the old silver train car.

There are about a dozen booths and a long counter. A lot of the seats are already taken, but there's still some room. I see the telephone against the far wall, not in use, waiting for me. But I can't just call somebody, can't just go from one world to the next in a split second. I'm not ready to go back to that other life yet, where people will be crying and thanking God and asking me a million questions I don't have answers for. It seems like days since I put on my jacket and ran down the front stairs of our house. It seems like that was a different person. I sit down at the counter between a man reading the newspaper and a woman in a jean jacket talking to her ten-year-old son on the next stool, trying to explain a math problem to him. Regular people, doing what they do every other day.

"Getcha something, hon?" a waitress with a ponytail asks me. "Coffee?"

"Um . . . yeah, coffee. And do you have . . . pancakes?" I'm so hungry, *starving*.

"Best on the North Shore. Blueberry or plain?"

"Blueberry."

"Bacon or sausage with that?"

"Sure," I say. "Bacon." Fat: my mother's enemy. I crave it.

The waitress yells my order down the counter to a man in a white T-shirt standing in front of a long, full grill. He nods in agreement, as if he approves of my choices. All of a sudden I feel terrifically happy, like nothing could ever go wrong in my life again. The waitress sets a mug of hot, hot coffee in front of me and I breathe it in.

"Don't burn yourself," she warns. What a wonderful place this is, where everyone takes care of you. I want to come back here all the time. I want to thank Leo for bringing me here, for showing me things I've never seen before.

Leo. Lee-O. The boy is Leo. I wonder where he is now? He was right not to tell me where he was going. I could tell someone. Oh, Leo, will I *have* to tell someone? If I tell my mother the truth, she'll certainly call the police and then they'll question me and everyone will get hysterical about it. Yes, I'll tell them, he *said* he would kill me, but he didn't. He didn't even really hurt me. He's not horrible—he just got messed up. But they won't hear that part. They won't believe me. They'll try to scare me, make me afraid of him again. They'll try to take Leo away from me.

I won't let them, though. When you make yourself real to somebody, they become real to you too. Even if you can't see them.

Leo. The police will want to know everything I know. What do I know? His name, but I won't admit that. I know he's large because of the coat. He has brown hair, soft brown hair. He does work that makes his hands greasy because the handkerchief had that smell. He lives in Fenton with his mother and sometimes his grandmother. His sister Michelle was killed four years ago by a man named Novack. I know too much. They could find him. I know too much.

So I won't tell. I sip my thick coffee and shudder. I know too much, but I don't know what I want to know. I don't know where to find him again. A tall boy with brown hair walks past the window and looks in. Maybe it's *him*. Maybe he's looking for me. But he keeps on walking.

A terrible thought occurs to me: If I saw him, I wouldn't know it. I'd have to listen to him, smell him, touch his hair.

The waitress sets a huge plate in front of me, a stack of pancakes, a mound of bacon, a beaker of syrup. "More coffee?" I nod. "If there's one thing I like to see, it's a girl who's not afraid of food!" she says, laughing. "Some of 'em act like it's gonna kill 'em to eat an egg. More power to ya, honey, more power to ya."

I smile back at her. I am powerful. I know that now.

There are old newspapers at the library. Four years ago yesterday. A murdered seventeen-year-old girl named Michelle. Her thirteen-year-old brother Leo. The papers would tell me who and where, the details I don't know.

I know enough. If I want to find Leo again, I can.

ELLEN WITTLINGER

is the author of the highly acclaimed teen novels *Razzle, What's in a Name, Hard Love* (an American Library Association Michael L. Printz Honor Book and a Lambda Literary Award winner), *Noticing Paradise,* and *Lombardo's Law,* as well as the middle-grade novel *Gracie's Girl.* She has a bachelor's degree from Millikin University in Decatur, Illinois, and an M.F.A. from the University of Iowa. A former children's librarian, she lives with her husband and two children in Swampscott, Massachusetts.

* * *